AIRSHIP 27 PRODUCTIONS

TM

The Wraith Volume One

"Just Who is The Wraith-Dread Avenger of the Underworld®?" ©2020 Frank Dirsherl
"Overlord of Under Town" ©2020 Bobby Nash
"The Warm Rush of Chilled Blood" ©2020 Greg Gick
"The Enemy Within" ©2020 Erik Franklin
"Sundown" ©2020 Frank Dirscherl & Adam Oravec

Published by Airship 27 Productions
www.airship27.com
www.airship27hangar.com

Interior illustrations © 2020 Chris Nye
Cover illustration © 2020 Adam Shaw

Editor: Ron Fortier
Associate Editor: Jaime Ramos
Marketing and Promotions Manager: Michael Vance
Production and design by Rob Davis

ISBN 978-1-946183-74-3

Printed in the United States of America

10 9 8 7 6 5 4 3 2 1

Contents

JUST WHO IS The Wraith- DREAD AVENGER OF THE UNDERWORLD ®?

Frank Dirscherl

I've been asked that question a lot over the last fifteen or so years, particularly at conventions and shows where I appear; but also online, via email and now through social media. Who is The Wraith? Where did he come from? Why did I create him or how did I think of him? The answer is both simple and complicated.

I created the character, oddly enough in my then backyard, back in 1998, as my answer to what I perceived was lacking in modern day comics at the time. By the late nineties, I was becoming disillusioned with comic books from the big publishers (that feeling has only increased since that time). I was to that point a lifelong reader and collector. During the seventies and eighties, I devoured comics from both DC and Marvel. I (or my family when I was really young) would buy just about everything. By the mid-nineties, though, comics really began to change. Story was no longer front and centre. It was now all about flashy (and oftentimes trashy) art that may (or may not) have looked pretty but just didn't advance the story in any way. Gimmicks became the go-to method to boost sales ("Things will never be the same again!"). Soap opera-style story antics (ignoring continuity, constantly rebooting titles over and over and over again) became the norm. By 1998, I was tired of it all. I remembered the stories of my youth, comics written by the likes of Denny O'Neil, Steve Englehart, Frank Robbins, Marv Wolfman, Bill Mantlo, Roy Thomas, John Byrne, Cary Bates, Gerry Conway, Roger Stern and many others. Art by the likes of Neal Adams, Marshall Rogers, Ernie Chua, Irv Novick, Gil Kane, Alex Saviuk, Carmine Infantino, George Perez, and many more. They created stories that were timeless, that can be read today and are still as effective, as evocative, as engaging as ever. The art produced wasn't just beautiful in its own right, but actually acted as an additional way to advance the story... as comic books are supposed to be. A cohesive partnership between writer and artist.

So, as I sat one day at home, I mused about a way to tell the stories of my youth, but with a character of my own design. One which had elements of the stories/characters I loved as a child (particularly Batman), but was still someone all my own. It was around this time that I discovered (through the magic of a then still-new invention called the Internet) pulp novels. The old classics, like the Shadow, Doc Savage and others. But especially what proved to be my favourite, the Spider - Master of Men. So, while my comic book thoughts bundled about in my mind, it occurred to me that I could also meld aspects of pulp characters such as the Spider into my own creation. Once that thought came to me, The Wraith was really born (and it's The Wraith, not The Wraith. I know it's technically wrong, but I chose to do it that way early on as a kind of marketing *schtick*, in the same way products on supermarket shelves are often spelled incorrectly. My thought was to try and make the character stand out as much as possible).

So, The Wraith really is a modern-day mix of old-style Batman comics and the Spider pulp novels. The stories themselves are really modern-day pulps in style and tone, albeit set in the present day, with the hero wearing a more comic book-style costume akin to the comics of old. The character is similar to those aforementioned heroes, in that he is a regular (though well trained) man, but with a twist. He is endowed with the powers of the Judgment Stare, which emanate from the Eyes of Judgment upon his chest, which force evildoers to feel the combined total of the pain and misery their crimes have inflicted on others, and which he received after a long trek in Africa. These powers, indeed the entire memories of the original Wraith/ Paul Sanderson, can be (and *were*) transferred to another deemed worthy in times of emergency. The (new) Wraith surrounds himself with a team- -his partner in life, Leena Patterson; his right-hand man, Max Horton; a butler, Jonathan Simpson; as well as a plethora of other agents that help from time-to-time. All the while battling such dastardly villains as crime lord Robert Latham, the Cobra (who played a large part in the original Wraith's origin), Natalya Blackova, Magnus Khan, Aztekoth, Dr Satanish and more. The parallels with Richard Wentworth, Nita van Sloan, Ram Singh/Ronald Jackson, and Jenkyns, and the Spider's grotesque gallery of nemeses, are there for all to see for anyone familiar with the genre.

And so, here we are in 2020. Several comics later, eight novels (with more to come), short stories, a myriad of merchandise (maquettes, action figures, t-shirts and the like). Even a live-action film! And now this anthology of short stories from Airship 27. I was super thrilled when Ron Fortier agreed to publish it. When it comes to modern-day pulp, he is **the** man. There is no finer exponent of the genre, no finer writer working in the field today, than Ron. I am honoured to have Airship 27 publish these stories, and even more honoured to have supplied two of them myself. My fellow storytellers—Greg Gick, Bobby Nash, Erik Franklin and

Adam Oravec—excelled themselves with their tales of mystery, action, excitement and daring-do. They are the best of the best. I hope you enjoy their stories as much as I did.

Take care.
Frank Dirscherl, Wollongong NSW, December 2019

Overlord of Under Town
Bobby Nash

A spotlight cut through the darkness like a knife.

Rick Mason was in a fog. His vision was blurred and each shaft of light he saw against the darkness that seemed to fill every nook and cranny of this place left streamers in his wake like something out of a movie. There was a sensation of moving, even though he could no longer feel his feet so he was unable to confirm that they were actually walking. Rough, callused hands pushed him along, slapping his back and pulling at his hair.

For the life of him, Rick, his friends all called him Mace because of his last name, had no idea how he had come to be in this place. It was like something out of a dream, a nightmare. Dark blocks made up the walls and ceiling. Where he touched them they felt slimy, as if they had been pulled from a creek bed our out of a fish tank. The smell of wet dirt mixed with a rancid smell that reminded him of the dumpster in the alley behind his apartment building. Congealed together, the sights and smells threatened to overwhelm his senses. It was all he could do to keep from throwing up.

From the amount of cotton that his throat felt like it swallowed, Mace assumed that he had tied one on real good the night before. He was doing that a lot of late. With the economy in the toilet, work was hard to find. It had been almost a year since he last punched a time clock and as much as he enjoyed not having to go to work every day, he did miss having a steady paycheck. He was behind on his rent, the cable had been turned off, and his cell phone no longer worked. The only credit he still had was his tab at the Old Scratch Bar down on West 81st Street. He'd been drinking there since his first fake ID in high school.

No amount of drinking, however, could explain how he ended up in some reject from an old horror movie set. From above he heard chants and shouts, but saw only darkness above.

A shove from behind sent him sprawling forward and he hit the sand covered floor with all the grace of a brick with wings. Even though every inch of him hurt, Mace found the strength to push himself up. Once he was back on unsteady legs he wiped away at the wet sand that stuck to him.

He looked into the blinding spotlight, squinting against the brightness.

"What the hell do you want?" he shouted to the mysterious man who he had spoken with earlier. He knew that he was in charge and would be watching from his perch above the arena, which is what he had called it. Or at least that's what he thought the man had said. It was all so hazy, blurry, and out of focus.

"I want nothing," a voice said from the darkness and all of the other voices went silent as their leader spoke. "You are merely... sport."

Mason was about to ask another question when he heard the turning of gears off to one side. The spotlight moved off of him. It tracked across the dirty floor to a gate that was rolling up along the side of the wall, raised by unseen hands pulling on a thick rope.

Like the spectators above, Mason stared in wonder as the gate revealed a tunnel much like the one he had entered through. Inside it was black as pitch, but somehow he knew that there was something inside.

When he heard the inhuman growl echo from the darkness he feared the worst.

Seconds, or was it minutes, he couldn't tell later something skittered out into the open arena. It was massive, but Rick Mason could only focus on rows of razor sharp teeth inside massive, powerful jaws.

If he were a praying man, he would have asked for a miracle to remove him from this place to a place of safety. But he was not a man of faith so instead he let loose a string of expletives that only resulted in howls of laughter from the crowd above.

"Any last words?" the man in the shadows asked.

"Yeah," Mace said then proceeded to tell the man to perform an anatomically impossible sex act with himself.

"How very predictable," the man in the shadows whispered, even though Rick Mason could not hear him.

Mace backed against the wall. He cast quick glances around the arena looking for any hint of a way out, but there was none. And he dared not take his eyes off the monster in front of him lest it move in for the kill.

The creature seemed content to wait him out, to play with his food, as it were. Mace wasn't all that eager to play this game, especially considering in which role he had been cast. "What are you waiting for?" he shouted at the beast.

The monster took the bait and surged forward at full speed, its mouth open wide.

He felt the heat of its breath and smelled the rancid scent of decay and death and found it fitting. The last things Rick Mason saw were the beast's powerful jaws flex and teeth coming right at his face.

He heard something pop.

And then there was nothing.

•••

Stuart Hanson was beginning to think that perhaps this wasn't a good idea.

Living in a crime-infested sewer like Metro City, a person got used to a certain amount of risk, especially if you went out after the sun set. It took a special kind of stupidity to wander the back streets of this gritty Gotham after midnight. Those who thought that Metro City was bad during the daylight hours would probably not be surprised to learn that it was even worse at night.

Stuart Hanson was your typical bully, and like most men in this position, he never thought he was in any danger. In high school he had been a king, quarterback for his state champion high school football team, which bought him a lot of latitude in spite of his less than average grades. It also won him a lot of points with the ladies. He never lacked for companionship. All that changed when he went to college and found out that he was no more special than the other high school recruits who were now his teammates and fiercest rivals, each of them with dreams of a multi-million dollar career in the NFL just like him.

Eventually the pressure became more than he could handle and he choked.

Then came a knee injury that he had been unable to recover from completely and his big league dreams of life on the football field were gone and he quickly found himself with no prospects.

Without football, his scholarship dried up and eventually he quit school and moved to Metro City in search of that fabled second chance the city's commercials and billboards were always promising. *Metro City: Where Second Chances Are Born.*

Sadly, that turned out to be a lie.

In Metro City, Stuart Hanson was still just a washed up football player with no skills and limited education. The only thing he had left was himself so he made it a point to keep his body in tip top shape. The knee eventually improved, although it never returned to full functionality and ached constantly so he took over the counter pain relief daily. Until they stopped working. Then he moved up to the high-end painkillers, but they weren't cheap and his minimum wage job barely covered the rent on his crappy one bedroom apartment and food. Still, the pain was constant and he eventually moved on to elicit drugs.

It wasn't long after that he began his career as a low rent B & E thug. Breaking and Entering was fairly easy and it helped him make enough money to stay pain free. At least for awhile. It wasn't until he was busted after robbing the wrong apartment and went to jail that he was able to get clean. It wasn't the ideal way to get off the drugs, but it was effective. The other good thing to come from his short stint upstate was that his time in the workout yard had gotten him back to peak physical shape. The knee was still an issue, but he was determined not to let it slow him down.

He was going to finally get that second chance to get his life back together.

Unfortunately, he was still a college drop out with no experience *and* now with a criminal record to boot. His job prospects were smaller than ever. Eventually, he found work at an auto repair machine shop. It turned out that he had an affinity for fixing broken machinery. His employer, an ex-con himself who had turned his life around after a stint in the joint, told him that he saw potential. He had even fronted him the money to enroll in night classes to improve his skills.

After classes, he liked to take a long walk to clear his thoughts. He was still in pretty descent shape, worked out regularly, took some martial arts classes, and occasionally did some boxing at the Y. Now that he had steady income, food in his belly, and a roof over his head, Stuart Hanson fell back into old habits. It wasn't the criminal behavior though. He stayed drug free and swore off his thieving ways. Hanson was still a bully though, just as he had been in high school. Everyone who knew him respected his power and most of them, at least the smart ones, knew to be intimidated by him, if not outright afraid.

He thought his reputation from having spent time on the insides would keep him safe on the cold and lonely streets of Metro City.

He was wrong.

Unfortunately for Stuart Hanson, the people who roamed the streets of Metro City in the wee hours of the morning were not the same ones who knew, or cared, about his reputation. Those who dwelled in the shadows of the city ate wannabe's like him for a late night snack and tossed away the rest for scraps.

Only two types roamed the Metro City streets after the witching hour.

Hunters.

And their prey.

His best friend, probably his only friend, Rick Mason had disappeared in this area a few days earlier. He wasn't really surprised that the police were doing nothing to find him. After all, what did they care if an ex-con disappeared in the slums of Metro City? Probably just one less problem they'd have to deal with later. Hanson assumed that all cops thought like that. He'd certainly never seen any evidence to the contrary. In fact, he had learned early on that the only person out there who would take care of Stuart Hanson was Stuart Hanson.

He didn't need anyone.

And he was quite all right with that.

•••

There were four of them.

From the look of them they were nothing more than four kids with attitude. When three of them came upon Stuart Hanson walking down Hutchinson Avenue, hands in his pockets in an effort to keep his hands warm, he almost laughed. They didn't look like much of a threat so Stuart was fairly certain he could take them. After all, what could a handful of kids know about fighting anyway?

He realized that there were four of them when the lead pipe struck him from behind. He fell forward, catching himself before he hit the ground and scratching the palms of his hands. He grit his teeth against the pain as one of them kicked him hard in the side and he thought he heard a rib crack. Blood poured from the cut on the back of his head.

They were laughing hard at the poor stupid man who had dared to walk into their territory. They joked and prodded, kicked and laughed. It was all a big joke to them. They were going to kill him and Stuart finally realized that they didn't care.

Suddenly he was afraid.

Fear spurred adrenaline and Stuart found a reservoir of strength. He swung out blindly, catching one of them off guard and knocking him to the ground with a bloody nose for his troubles. The others took a cautious step back.

Stuart saw his opening and he bolted through it. He had gotten at least ten steps ahead of them by the time they realized that he was making a run for it and gave chase. Fueled by a burst of adrenaline, Stuart had a commanding lead, but they were closing the gap quickly. And they knew the area a lot better than he did.

Stuart turned down a side street in the hopes of finding a place to hide or maybe yell for help where someone might hear him. His hopes were shattered, however, when he realized that it wasn't a side street that he had turned into. It was a blind alley with only one way in or out.

And four very angry young men were blocking it.

The giant graffiti scrawled DEAD END inside a circle with a line through it mocked him. Beneath the sign was a tag that read WELCOME TO UNDER TOWN in big letters that looked like they were melting, the colors running down the wall toward the concrete street. The painted brick wall had no windows and the only light in the alley came from a street lamp near the entrance that cast a pale yellow glow over everything inside. Aside from all of that, even Stuart had to admit that the artist that had tagged the wall was rather talented.

Four shadows appeared like apparitions against the wall.

"Looks like you made a wrong turn, mister," the young man with the bloody nose sneered from the mouth of the alley, the pale yellow light behind him casting the shadows of him and his friends over the alley and everything in it.

Stuart Hanson was sweating. The last thing he wanted was to get his ass kicked by a bunch of hooligans, but he'd be damned if he were going to just stand there and take a beating. If nothing else, they were going to have to work for it. He settled into a fighting stance that he had learned in one of his lessons, which only made the four teens burst out in a fit of laughter. Not that it mattered to him. They could laugh all they wanted, but he wasn't going down without a fight.

"Bring it," Stuart Hanson said through fear induced arrogance. Math wasn't his strong suit, but even he knew that the odds were against him. He figured he could take a couple of them though. They would know they had been in a fight.

His bloody nosed friend snapped open a switchblade knife and took a step forward. "Oh, I'm going to enjoy this," he said and stepped into the alley.

At that moment, Stuart Hanson knew he was a dead man.

●●●

The Wraith patrolled Metro City.

It was all but impossible for him to cover the same sectors every night.

Metro City was massive and more than one man could keep an eye on alone. Of course, he had help. He had been slowly setting up a network of people, shop owners, cops, housewives, and transit workers who uploaded any suspicious behavior they noticed to a secure website. None of them knew that The Wraith was the one receiving this information, but it had helped him keep a better watch on this city that he loved.

There were, of course, exceptions to every rule and the particular part of town he was in at that moment certainly fell into that category. Normally, The Wraith kept his patrol route random enough that no one could predict where or when he might show up. When trouble did rear its ugly head, The Wraith was there to smack it atop its evil little head. This area was the exception. He made it a point to be seen in the area at least once a night. Just to let them know he was around.

Things had actually been rather quiet of late, which made him a bit uncomfortable. It was cliche to call these rare moments of peace *the calm before the storm*, but bitter experience taught him that there was truth in the description.

This part of the city was always a sore spot for him. It had been dubbed as Under Town by many and the nickname stuck. No one called this area by its designated name any longer. No matter how hard he, or even the authorities, tried, there never seemed to be anything but violence in Under Town. Just a few weeks back a family had been gunned down not far away, their only child the sole survivor. A couple of miles away, an arsonist had emptied an entire city block so that an unscrupulous businessman could scoop up the land for pennies on the dollar. He was currently in jail, thanks to The Wraith's intervention while a non-profit group headed up by his alter ego, Paul Sanderson, worked to reclaim the area and build affordable housing units. So far it was an uphill battle, but he was determined to see the project succeed.

In recent weeks there had been a rash of petty thefts of stores that were closed at night. Someone had taken enough groceries to feed a small army. Homeless men and women lined many of the stoops of Under Town, just looking for a place to grab a few hours of sleep without being noticed by any of the number of predators that prowled these streets. Random violence was not unheard of here.

The Wraith had made Under Town a permanent stop on his patrol, but sometimes he wondered if it was enough. He had been working on a plan with Leena and Max for an increased presence in the area, but so far hadn't been able to make it happen. Even he, for all of his resources, couldn't be everywhere at once.

Tonight's patrol had been more or less routine for Under Town. He'd stopped a few petty robberies, and stopped a fight a few blocks over. He was just about to call it a night and head back home when he caught sight of a foot chase on Hutchinson Avenue. He recognized the man being chased. He had seen him out walking the streets earlier in the evening. Although it had seemed odd that anyone would be foolish enough to go for a walk at this hour alone in Metro City, this was still a free country. From the look of things, the walker had run across some unfriendlies.

The Wraith didn't recognize the youths, but they were obviously street toughs of some kind. They weren't wearing the colors of any gang he had run across so that probably meant they were new in town.

He smiled.

The Wraith liked introducing himself to the new scumbags that came to his city.

They were chasing a man he didn't know. Perhaps this man had simply picked the wrong street to walk down and unintentionally entered their territory. It certainly wouldn't be the first time something like that had happened. Gang wars had been started over far less. It had happened before and something told him that this probably wouldn't be the last time it did either. At least this time The Wraith could do something about it.

I guess it's time I said hello, he thought.

The Wraith stepped to the edge and then over it as if gravity was not a concern.

●●●

Stuart Hanson was confused when the approaching toughs stopped short. For a moment, just a moment, he allowed himself the self delusion that they had realized that he was not a man with which to mess and were rethinking their plan to do just that. Of course, that notion was quickly dismissed the second he saw the caped figure vault past him.

The newcomer was a blur of black and blue as he took down the first of the street fighters with a single left hook. A second hit knocked another on his butt seconds later.

For a moment, Hanson contemplated sticking around to watch the show. Like everyone else in Metro City, he had heard the rumors of a vigilante in a cape and mask who stalked the streets at night. There was no proof of this masked man, though, only a whispered name. They called this vigilante The Dread Avenger of the Underworld and his exploits, whether real or imagined, painted a clear image of a dangerous vigilante roaming the streets looking for criminals. Hanson had not been a believer in this boogey man, believing him to be nothing more than an urban legend started by meth heads whose burnt out brains cells had cooked up to explain their bad trip.

He had assumed that this Dread Avenger character was probably made up by the same people that told him about the cultists that had once called Metro City home.

But now…

Now Stuart Hanson was a believer.

The guy in the cape had caught the four gang-bangers by surprise, but he was still outnumbered four to one. Plus, he really had no way of knowing whether or not the newcomer would be any better or worse than the four surly teenagers that had chased him into the alley to begin with. If the rumors were true, The Wraith was a stone-cold killer. If you were on the wrong side of his law then you were dead.

Getting out of there was his best bet, he decided.

There was just one problem. He was in a dead end alley and the fight was between him and the exit. There was no way he was going to slip past them without getting caught up in the free for all that was happening just a few feet away from him. It hadn't taken long for it to go from a fistfight to a knife fight as weapons were drawn. How long, Hanson wondered, before one of them produced a gun and started shooting? He would rather not be there when that happened.

"This is not good," he muttered even as he looked for an exit. He felt along the wall, especially the parts hidden in shadow. Surely there had to be some kind of door, window, or even a laundry shoot he could squeeze through.

There wasn't.

He couldn't even find a fire escape ladder so he could climb above the melee.

"Crap!" he cursed as he hit the wall in frustration.

He heard a roar that echoed off the brick walls. He turned his gaze skyward, scanning the rooftops for any indication that's where the noise came from. Whatever had made the sound was undoubtedly bigger, meaner, and angrier than the guys fighting it out at the mouth of the alley to see which one of them gets to take him on next.

Something brushed past his leg in the dark. He couldn't see anything, but it was there. That's when he felt something grab him around the ankles, another arm wrapped around his leg. The hands that grabbed at him pulled and Hanson lost his balance and fell forward. He hit the ground hard and saw stars and explosions of light from the impact of his head bouncing off the dirty concrete that made up the alley's floor.

The world spun around him at a dizzying pace. It was all he could do not to throw up all over himself. He heard a rumble beneath him and another tug at his legs. That's when the ground opened up beneath him and darkness swallowed him whole.

Stuart Hanson tried to scream as he was dragged into the darkness below.

●●●

The Wraith was impressed.

It was fairly obvious from their moves that none of his opponents had professional training but what they lacked in style, they more than made up for in speed, exuberance, and raw power. None of them had pulled a single punch, a consideration he had been affording them. There was little doubt that he could take them, but it would take time and the last thing he needed was for the cops to arrive and catch The Wraith in the middle of a brawl in a dark alley. They would most likely come in with guns blazing. *Shoot first and ask questions later* was becoming an all too frequent motto for Metro City's police force, especially when dealing with Under Town.

Besides, he needed to find the man these guys had been chasing. The loud roar they had all heard had halted the fight, but only for a moment. The Wraith saw the man drop, but didn't have the opportunity to leap to his aid because the four men decided to attack again. The Wraith spun around and placed a boot into the chest of one of his attackers, pinning him to the chipped brick. At first he wasn't sure if he'd seen what he thought because he was otherwise engaged with the fight. It was possible that the man had simply stumbled and fell into the shadows and was still lying there, hidden by the darkness. Something told him that wasn't the case though. And he still couldn't explain the roar.

He had to hand it to the kids. They had stamina. He'd knocked each of them down at least twice and they were all back on their feet in a flash and still ready to trade punches again.

Until the sound of a police siren pierced the night.

They ran.

STUART HANSON TRIED TO SCREAM...

The Wraith started to give chase, but thought better of it, especially once he saw them split off into different directions once they reached the street that intersected the mouth of the alley. He wasn't worried about them getting away. They had struck him as the arrogant sort and they were local. He knew their paths would cross again soon. Right now he had to figure out what happened to their victim.

"It's all right now," he called out to the darkened alley just in case the man was simply hiding in the shadows. "It's safe! They're gone!"

The only sound was the siren growing louder.

"Hello?" he called again. "Where are you?"

The Wraith walked deeper into the alley, a small flashlight in his hand. He was constantly amazed at how often he found himself in dark alleys, abandoned tenement buildings, or some other place that shied away from working light fixtures so he was always prepared with a flashlight. The night vision in his cowl worked wonders, but there was just enough light in the alley to make their use problematic.

"Where are you?" he asked, this time not expecting an answer. The light played across the ground and against the brick wall. There was no sign of the man he had seen chased into this alley. He went to the area where he had last seen the man. With his boot, The Wraith pushed aside the loose papers that littered the alley. There was a manhole cover there, large enough for the man to easily fit through. He pulled against the steel cover, but it wouldn't budge.

"Hmmm..." he thought and tapped on it with his foot. It seemed solid so he put his full weight on it. Still nothing.

"This doesn't make any sense," he mumbled to himself. The manhole cover was positioned an arm's length from the wall, which was weird. Ordinarily, the Metro City Water and Power Works crews installed manholes in the center of the street so they could have plenty of room to bring in equipment as needed. A hole this close to a wall didn't make sense. There was also a small spatter of blood near the cover. *He must have hit his head when he fell*, The Wraith decided. A dragging pattern from the spatter to the manhole cover filled in the remaining blanks. The Wraith tugged at the manhole cover, but it would not budge. Even as heavy as they were, he had hefted his fair share of covers. This one gave no indication of lifting out of its groove.

He played the beam of light over the wall until he noticed something odd. "What's this?" he said, ignoring the approaching sirens. One of the bricks looked different than the others and he stepped closer to the wall for a better look. "One of these things is not like the others," The Wraith whispered, quoting a famous children's program. "One of these things does not belong."

He reached out and pushed against the brick and felt it give as it slid into the wall.

The manhole cover slid open like a trap door.

The Wraith smiled.

"I love this city," he said. "It never ceases to surprise me." He played the beam inside the hole and saw the ladder that went down at least several feet. Without a second thought, The Wraith found himself scurrying down the ladder into the waiting unknown.

He was about two feet down the ladder when the manhole cover automatically slid back into place overhead just as red and blue flashes of light filled the alley above.

And then there was only darkness.

●●●

The ladder ended eight feet below the surface into a sewer tunnel. The Wraith dropped the final three feet to the concrete floor, causing a cloud of dust to billow up around him. He tensed, ready for an attack. When it was clear that none was forthcoming, he played his light along the empty corridor. Once he was certain he was alone, The Wraith activated the night vision goggles in his cowl and knelt next to two tracks indented in the dust. Another small dribble of blood was there as well. The man's injury was minor and the bleeding was already beginning to stop.

The man I'm looking for did come down here, the Wrath thought as he followed the trail made by the feet of a person being dragged away. *But he wasn't so fortune to find it empty.*

The Wraith followed the trail deeper into the tunnel. There was only a trickle of water in this part of the sewer system, which made it a perfect place for the homeless to seek refuge from the elements, especially now that cooler was weather was in the forecast. There had even been a rumor of possible snow flurries within the next three to five days. When the temperature dropped, Metro City's less fortunate moved underground.

"So where are they?" The Wraith wondered. The sewer tunnel continued on without so much as a hint of anyone there. *Curious*, he thought, but pressed on. His primary goal was to find the missing man from the alley. He would worry about the rest after he was sure the man was safe.

Finally, he came to a T-junction where the tunnel intersected another tunnel. There were three choices: go back the way he came, which wasn't really an option, go left, or go right. The tracks in the dust went off to the right so that's the way The Wraith went as well. The sound of rushing water was louder this way and it wasn't long until he found himself walking across a thin concrete wall that ran along the center of the tunnel, just an inch or two above the water. It wasn't much farther beyond that before the water level rose again and he was knee deep in the freezing cold water. His suit was insulated so The Wraith was able to withstand the cold water longer than he would without such considerations. Still, despite this advantage he needed to get out of the water as soon as possible. His feet were already beginning to go numb from the extreme temperatures.

The Wraith grabbed hold of the first ladder he saw on his right and climbed out of the water. He paused and sat in the smaller tunnel for a moment to catch his breath. Only a small trickle flowed through this tunnel and he saw a light of some kind at the far end of it. He started to move forward when he heard a sound. He stopped and listened carefully, but couldn't make out the cause of the noise. It reminded him of the sound a cat made when it walked across tin. The sound of claws tapping on a hard surface.

The Wraith stared into the tunnel and two yellow orbs glowed against the darkness of the tunnel. Something was approaching fast, moving through the tunnel quickly and bearing down on his position. He had heard the stories of monsters in the sewer, of course. Every major city in the United States, if not the world, had similar tales of creatures that lived underground. He had seen many things since he first donned the costume of The Wraith, but even he had never believed that giant alligators roamed the sewers beneath Metro City.

Until he saw one bearing down on him.

The gator's mouth was open and a roar emanated from its gullet as it came at him.

All The Wraith saw were teeth. Big, sharp teeth.

He braced himself, ready to move at just the right moment. Timing would be tricky, but there was no way he could outrun the monster. That much was clear from seeing how fast it moved through the tunnel toward him. He planted his feet and held on to the iron hand rails that ran along the top of the tunnel to prevent slipping. With snapping jaws only a few inches from him, The Wraith kicked back from the opening and together he and the alligator that saw him as its next meal were airborne.

The Wraith held firm to the handhold as the giant scaled creature plowed into him at full speed. It was almost like being run over by a mid-sized automobile, which had happened to him once upon a time while trying to catch a killer who had run into oncoming traffic. He felt the creature's scaly hide tear away pieces of his costume, some of the gouges drawing blood. His muscles ached and he heard a pop in his shoulder and pain screamed through his entire body.

He lost his grip.

Together, The Wraith and the alligator fell into the rushing water below. Then sank beneath the icy current.

●●●

Massive jaws snapped shut just centimeters from the Dread Avenger of the Underworld's face, but The Wraith held tight to the alligator's neck. Or at least what he thought of as the creature's neck. He had read once that to corral a snake and keep it from biting you all you had to do was grab it behind the head where it could not swivel around and bite you and hold it with enough force to immobilize the head. It sounded easy in theory, but he'd seen snakes move rather quickly. Grabbing it was the truly tricky part.

The alligator was much the same. Hitting the freezing water was a shock to his system, but not as much as it might have been if he wasn't already cold and wet from his earlier dip. The gator was right at home in the water, but it too was dazed from the fall. The Wraith moved quickly, fueled by adrenaline and, he wasn't afraid to admit it, a healthy dose of fear. The alligator made a move for him and The Wraith was able to kick off from the tunnel wall just ahead of rows of teeth that could have ripped him to shreds. The gator's snout hit the wall at full speed, which gave The Wraith a very brief window to enact his crazy plan.

He leapt onto the alligator's back and wrapped his arms around it tightly. His cape was in his right hand and he grabbed it with his left to pull around like a lasso or a rein. If worse came to worst, he would use the cape to try to strangle the alligator. Like every other creature, The Wraith assumed that the alligator needed to breathe to remain conscious. Or so he hoped.

It was moments like these where he wished he had paid better attention in biology class. The only thing he knew about alligators was that they had powerful jaws, were fast, and one of them had bitten off Captain Hook's hand in Peter Pan. Or was that a crocodile? He couldn't recall.

All of these thoughts blasted through his brain as he tried to hold tight to the thrashing creature beneath him. The gator was tough, no doubt about it. It was also more at home in the water then The Wraith was so it had a distinct advantage. His mind raced through possible scenarios for knocking out the creature, but smoke bombs and gas grenades weren't very effective underwater.

The alligator thrashed again and The Wraith felt the jarring impact of his back against the concrete wall of the sewer tunnel as the beast tried to dislodge him. A second impact knocked the breath from him and he gasped as fetid water filled his throat and lungs. With the third impact his head cracked into the wall and his grip loosened. Suddenly free of its attacker, the alligator spun around as if unaffected by the current and swam toward its target.

Too stunned to think straight, The Wraith sank toward the bottom, unable to breathe. Images of Leena Patterson flashed before him and it made him smile. Never before had he ever felt such love for an individual as he felt for her. She was his rock, his life. He wasn't afraid of dying, but not seeing Leena again made him ache inside. He felt something tug at his shoulders. Whatever it was, it pulled him against the current, against gravity, lifted him up toward the surface. He tried to help, to kick out with his feet and swim for the safety, but his legs refused to move.

The monster's roar mixed with the roar of the flowing water and the thundering of his heart in his ears was deafening to the point of being overwhelming. He wanted to scream, to add his fury to the chorus all around him, but there was no air left in his lungs, only a burning sensation of rising bile.

That's when his vision blurred around the edges as the jaws of death bore down on him in shades of eerie green from the night vision goggles.

I hope you choke on me, you bastard, was his last thought before he passed out.

•••

The first thing he heard was voices.

They were muffled, but there was no mistaking the fear in them. He tried to move, to sit up, but every muscle in his body hurt from the effort. All he wanted to do was lie there with his eyes closed until the pain went away. Unfortunately, the thought of a nap was a luxury he couldn't afford.

"He's awake," one of the muffled voices said.

"Barely," The Wraith muttered unintelligibly. He was face down on a cold hard surface that smelled of mold and old socks. It took some effort, but he somehow managed to lift himself up enough to roll over onto his back. His cape, still wet from the deluge, stuck to his legs. "Where am I?" he asked, although he couldn't be certain it had come out resembling any kind of English.

"Rest easy, my friend," a soft voice said from nearby. A shuffling sound caught his ear. He heard the owner of the voice as he approached and knelt beside him. Something touched his lips. "Here. Drink this," the soothing voice said.

He did as instructed. He took a sip of the fresh, cold water; and then coughed uncontrollably, losing most of the water.

"Easy," the voice said. "Easy. Slow sips."

"Th--thank you," The Wraith stammered as he pushed himself into a seated position. It hurt, but he opened his eyes and was nearly blinded. He reached up and turned off the night vision and the green and white halo around everything disappeared. "Who are you?" he asked the man kneeling next to him.

"I was about to ask you the same thing," the man said, offering a slight smile that seemed out of place on his dirt-crusted face. The clothes he wore were also dirty, frayed at the edges as if he" been wearing it awhile. The gloves on his hand were so old that they no longer covered his fingers.

The others were dressed similarly, The Wraith noted. There were easily twenty of them ranging in age from eighteen to forty. They were all thin, probably malnourished, he assumed. His first thought was that they were homeless and had moved underground as the cooler weather of winter approached.

"They call me The Wraith."

"An unusual name," the man said. He lifted up the edge of his wet cape. "I guess that makes sense considering your unusual clothes."

The Wraith chuckled. "My work clothes do look pretty strange sometimes, but it has its uses as well."

"If you say so," the man said. He held out a hand. "My name is William. William Lassiter."

"Nice to meet you, Mr. Lassiter," he shook the offered hand. "I assume I have you to thank for my rescue?"

Lassiter pointed to a couple of young men standing nearby. "It was Andrew and Frank who found you. It was they who saved you from certain death."

"Ol' Jake was about ready to take a big bite out of you, mister," one of the men said.

"I'm Frank, by the way." He nodded.

The Wraith returned the nod. "You named that thing Jake?"

"What would you call him?"

"Godzilla," The Wraith said, only half joking.

Most of the others laughed.

"So ol' Jake is a pet then?" The Wraith asked.

"Not exactly," Lassiter said. "More like a neighbor. We have an understanding, right Frank?"

"An understanding? Really?"

"Sure," Frank said. "We stay out of his way and he doesn't try to eat us."

"Sounds like a smart plan," The Wraith agreed.

"It's worked for us so far," Lassiter added.

"Regardless, I'm in your debt. Thanks."

"You a cop?" the other young man who he assumed was Andrew said, interrupting before anyone else could say anything. His voice was angry and he was one of the few that hadn't laughed at the new arrival's attempt at humor.

"No. Not a cop."

"A super villain then?" Lassiter asked, one eyebrow raised as he held up the edge of the cape.

"I guess that depends on who you ask," The Wraith laughed. But for Andrew's angry expression, he added, "Relax. I'm no super villain either."

"Then what exactly are you?" the young man's fists were balled at his side, a tremor running through them. It wouldn't take much to spring him to violence. The Wraith realized he had to tread smoothly.

"I'm one of the good guys."

Andrew shot him a look that told The Wraith that the young man did not believe him so he tried another tact.

"I'm a concerned citizen who loves his city and will do whatever it takes to keep it safe." He pointed to the cowl he wore. "Even if it means dressing up and crawling around back alleys."

"You'll have to excuse Andrew," Lassiter said. "We don't get many strangers down here, but when we do they aren't generally friendly."

"I understand," The Wraith said as he got to his feet, one hand against the wall to help keep his balance. "Trust me, I'm not here to bother you. As I said, I was looking for a man. He fell down a hole. Anyone here seen him?"

A chorus of no's and head shakes answered.

"How long have you been down here, Mr. Lassiter?"

"A SUPER VILLAIN THEN?"

"Not long. We move around a lot."

"I see."

A veil of sadness darkened the man's face. "No you don't," he said, just barely above a whisper.

"You're right. I don't. How did you end up living down here?"

Lassiter shrugged. "It's the same old story. I worked for a company for fifteen years. I rarely missed a day, worked overtime and weekends, and then one day they decided to outsource my job and laid me off. Now I can't find work because the job market is *weak*, to use a term I've heard a lot. Some HR folks have even told me that they won't hire me because I worked for my last company as long as I did." He tried to laugh it off, but The Wraith could see the man's disappointment. It wasn't a large leap from disappointed to angry. "I remember a time when employers appreciated loyalty and stable workers. I guess I didn't change with the times, huh?"

"I know that feeling," The Wraith said.

"I got some help," Lassiter continued. "I'm not too proud to accept help when I need it, but eventually it ran out and I lost my home, my marriage crumbled, and I had nowhere else to go so I ended up here."

"I'm sorry."

"Nothing to be sorry for, my friend. It's not your fault."

"Regardless, I still feel terrible."

"I appreciate that," Lassiter smiled. "We've got a fire going in the next alcove. You're welcome to share it until you dry out."

The Wraith was impressed that he could smile and have concern for a total stranger when it would be so easy to wallow in self-pity and anger. He was starting to like William Lassiter. He was a true leader.

"Thank you, I appreciate it."

"If you'll follow me."

Lassiter motioned the direction and The Wraith fell in line with him as they walked along the edge of the tunnel in a small pathway above the water line. The others fell into step behind him with Andrew immediately following. The Wraith got the sense that the young man still didn't trust him. Not that he could blame him. If a masked man showed up on the doorstep of Sanderson House he would probably be skeptical as well.

What the dread avenger did not know was that other, more sinister eyes were watching them.

But he would soon find out.

●●●

"Do you have any idea what's going on here, partner?" Rosa Perez asked as she ducked beneath the yellow crime scene tape that the uniformed MPD officer held up for her. She had a notebook and small pen light in one hand and a steaming hot paper cup of coffee in the other. She did not look happy.

"Just the usual," Detective Bob Sloan said. "Vigilante gang violence at its finest."

Perez rolled her eyes in that *here we go again* way she always did when her partner was getting ready to launch into one of his tirades on any number of topics of which he claimed to be an expert. Vigilantes, and more specifically, the so-called Wraith, were always high on his list of things to complain about these days.

Sloan must have noticed. "What?" he asked.

"Did I say anything?" Perez said with a playful smile.

"You didn't have to."

"Well there you go then," she said before taking a sip of her coffee. "So, why am I up before the sunshine this fine early morning?"

"Like I said," her partner started.

"Vigilante gang violence at its finest," they continued in unison. Sloan was a topnotch detective, but once he glommed onto something he was like a bulldog with a bone. There would be no getting it away from him until he was ready to let it go on his own. He was nowhere near ready to let The Wraith go.

"Uniforms responded to a domestic violence call. Reports stated that there was some kind of brouhaha in the alley and there were sightings of a guy with a cape. Sound familiar?"

"Is there a victim?"

"Not exactly."

"Not exactly? What does *not exactly* mean?"

Sloan pointed with his flashlight to an area near the wall. "We've got blood. Not a lot of it, but it's fresh."

Perez squatted near the blood. "I bleed more than this if I cut myself shaving," she said. "We've got no vic, Sloan."

"Not yet."

"And just where do you suggest we look?"

Detective Sloan didn't have an answer for that one.

"Come on," Detective Perez said. "Let's work the scene and see what a canvas turns up. If there's something here then we'll move on it."

"And if there's nothing?" Sloan asked as he watched his partner duck back under the crime scene tape and head back to her car.

"Then I'm going back home and going to bed."

●●●

The Wraith knew something was wrong before it happened. He had been at this business for a long time and had learned the hard and painful way to trust his instincts. And when those instincts started screaming that something was wrong he knew better than to ignore it.

The attack was fast and furious and came from the shadows. The first salvo consisted of arrows fired by archers he couldn't see. The arrows were wide, sparking off walls where they hit. To the untrained eye, it would appear as though the attackers were not very proficient with their weapons, but The Wraith knew that it took just as much skill for a true professional to miss on purpose than it did to find his mark. The arrows were doing what they were supposed to accomplish.

They were herding Lassiter and his people where the bad guys wanted them to go.

"Stop!" The Wraith shouted, but no one listened. Panic surged all around him as the underground dwellers pushed their way through the archway up ahead. "Stop!" he shouted again, but to no avail. *It's a bottleneck!* He knew it was a trap, but Lassiter and his people were survivors, not fighters. They did not see it the same way he did so they were blundering right into the obvious trap.

Sure enough, the net on the other side of the archway fell upon the small group and was cinched tight by unseen hands that were waiting on the other side. A few of them tried to fight, especially young Frank and angry Andrew, but they were overwhelmed. They were then tossed into the back of a cage that looked like something out of an old movie set in Victorian times.

"Hey!" The Wraith shouted a split second before he slammed into one of the attackers, catching him by surprise. A series of quick strikes and The Wraith lowered his unmoving body to the cold, wet floor.

But he wasn't alone.

The villain had a friend nearby who came at The Wraith with a machete. The Wraith backpedaled to stay out of the reach of the man's blade. There wasn't a lot of room to move in the tunnel and The Wraith had the added limitation of not knowing the intricate tunnel system beneath Metro City. That put him at an immediate disadvantage so ending the fight quickly was his best bet.

The man with the machete had youth and knowledge of his surroundings on his side, but he wasn't a trained combatant. His moves were raw and undisciplined. He simple swung with all his might, hacking at his intended target. The Wraith parried, dodged, and danced around the flashing blade until he saw his opening. He slammed his gloved hands together, trapping the blade between them and held it tight. He pulled the blade forward, which caught his attacker off guard and he tripped and fell forward.

Right into The Wraith's waiting knee. The dread avenger caught him with an uppercut and he heard teeth slam together and the man's grip on the machete loosened. A quick chop to the right spot on the back of the neck and the man was lying unconscious at his feet.

He was about to go after the folks caught in the net when a movement to the left caught his attention. The Wraith spun just in time to see a set of massive jaws snapping in his direction. He recoiled on instinct, backpedaling away from the mighty muscled snappers of the alligator that bore down on him. *Not this again*, he thought before he realized that this was not the same creature he had faced before. This one was smaller, but just as fast and apparently just as angry.

It was all so surreal to him. A fully functioning society living beneath the streets, traps and buggies with kidnap victims, giant monster alligators, and swords and machetes. The only thing needed to complete the illusion was a mustache-twirling villain.

The Wraith kept a selection of defensive weaponry in his utility belt. He pulled three small marble sized steel balls from a pouch, never taking his eyes off the beast that was slowly stalking toward him, an impossibly sick smile creasing its cracked and worn snout.

He tossed the marbles toward the alligator and prayed that they still worked despite the dunking he'd taken earlier. The balls bounced one, twice, then a third time before the familiar snap-hiss filled the air as the compressed gasses inside the pellet balls released and filled the air with a gray-tinted haze.

The beast roared and increased its speed, charging ahead. The Wraith braced himself, ready to break left or right depending on the monster's next action. The gator was close, too close, when it stopped.

And collapsed, unconscious, to the cold stone.

The Wraith breathed a sigh of relief. Going toe to toe with one of those giant killers was bad enough. Two would have been pushing it. He was just glad that the knockout gas actually worked on the alligator.

There was no time to rest on his laurels, however. William Lassiter and his people were in trouble. The Wraith ran through the archway in pursuit, ready for whoever was on the other side ready to spring their trap and catch him.

Unfortunately, there was no one waiting for him on the other side. Whoever had attacked them had taken Lassiter and his people and The Wraith had no idea which tunnel they had taken. From where he stood there were three possible directions they could have gone.

"Blast it!" he shouted angrily.

The Wraith needed a plan. *Or a hound dog*, he thought before snapping his fingers as an idea struck him. It was crazy, but he was quickly running out of options. Somehow, the bad guys, whoever they were, had found a way to control the alligators. That was the only scenario that made sense to explain why the beast came in with them and attacked only The Wraith and not any of the slower potential victims. He would have thought it impossible, but he couldn't discount what he had witnessed with his own eyes.

Somewhere out there in the maze of tunnels beneath Metro City was a man or woman holding the beast's leash. And that person was at the end of one of three connecting tunnels. He started to pick one at random and hope for the best, but dismissed that notion as quickly as he had it. If he picked the wrong one, then the odds of finding Lassiter and his people lessened and that was unacceptable.

What The Wraith needed was a plan.

The idea came to him unbidden, almost like the cliche light bulb blinking into existence above his head. "Of course," he muttered, snapping gloved fingers.

Now that he had a plan, The Wraith decided to turn that control back on this mystery villain.

He took position in the shadows, careful to remain out of sight. He pulled a couple of metal pellets from a different pouch, colored blue. "I can't believe I'm doing this," he muttered just seconds before tossing the blue pellets toward the sleeping alligator. Like the previous ones used to take out the monster, the pellets bounced three times on the hard concrete before settling in front of the snoring beast. A snap-hiss and a stream of white vapor shot into the air around the alligator, who breathed it in deeply. The gas acted quickly as the beast began to stir. Then it shook its head back and forth as it to shake loose the cobwebs of a deep sleep. The Wraith recognized the motion. He often felt like that when Leena tried to wake him each afternoon. Unlike himself, however, the alligator seemed to wake up far faster.

From his perch in the shadows, The Wraith watched the alligator skitter through the archway and head off into one of the tunnels. He noted that when he was planning to pick a tunnel at random this was not the one he would have chosen. Once the critter had gotten a good clip down the tunnel, The Wraith stepped out of his hiding place and followed, careful not to alert the beast to his presence.

Wherever it was headed, it wasn't in any big hurry. The Wraith just hoped it led him where he wanted to go.

●●●

Stuart Hanson screamed and was rewarded with a painful punch to the midsection that brought him to his knees.

The hard, uneven concrete was hard, cold, and covered in a thin film of slime, a side effect of the stagnant water pooled all over the small cavern-like room he'd been dragged into. Arched columns made of the same dark stained blocks of granite marked the entrance to each of the three tunnels that fed the cavern. Despite being underground, he was surprised by the high walls and tall ceiling.

"On your feet!" the beefy man who had punched him snarled. He wouldn't call their interactions a conversation, but so far everything he'd said had been with a snarl. He reminded Stuart of Bluto from the old Popeye cartoons.

"Where are we--"

Before he could finish, Bluto jerked him to his feet and pushed him forward in the direction of the archway in the center. To the left and right he could hear running water, or at least it sounded that way. With every sound echoing off the stone walls, he couldn't be completely certain of anything except that he was pretty sure he was about to die. The fight in the alley, which seemed a lifetime ago, was far less terrifying.

Once he passed through the arch, there were cloths hanging like drapes. He passed through several, pushing through them face first since Bluto had securely tied his hands behind his back. The cloth was damp and smelled very much like a wet dog. After the fourth curtain he stepped into a well-lit room. Like the other rooms he'd seen since they crossed the rushing water and took a flight of steep stairs down into this strange world he never could have dreamed existed, this one was made of the same stones that were dark from moisture age. The light came from several lamps scattered about the room. In the center of the room was a fire pit, also made from the same granite rocks. A fire crackled and popped in the pit, creating shadows to play along the walls. Nearby was another ditch filled with flowing water, but moving much slower than the one a level above.

The heat of the fire was welcome. He'd been cold from the moment he picked himself up from the floor of the tunnel where he fell in. He scrambled closer to the fire, careful that Bluto not mistake his desire for warmth for trying to make a run for it. He was almost to the center of the room by the time he realized that there was another big difference between this room and the others.

This room was occupied.

Stuart Hanson froze when he heard the hiss. It felt out of place in a place like this. When he realized that there was no monster just waiting to leap out of the darkness and devour him, he relaxed slightly and turned his head to look around the room. There were men and women lining the far wall, each of them looked as if they were in dire need of a bath, and maybe a little time in the sun. Or a tanning bed. None of them looked too all fired impressed with him either.

There was a large chair on the other side of the fire. It was the most ornate thing in the room and there were two flickering torches on poles, one on each side of the chair that made it scream to be called a throne. There was a man sitting casually on the throne with one knee draped over the other, but Stuart only paid him a cursory glance. His gaze fixated on the two mammoth alligators that filled the space on each side of the throne, their tails swishing back and forth along the floor creating the hissing sound he had heard.

Each monster was attached to a chain that looked too thin to handle them should they have decided to make a break for it. The man on the throne held the other end of the chains in his grizzled hand. In the other hand he held a smelly cigar.

"Welcome," the man said. His voice cracked, probably from a combination of smoking plus the respiratory problems living in such a damp environment had probably caused. He was dressed in nice clothing, far less dirty and tattered than the others that were scattered about the room were. He also had the distinction of being washed and groomed.

"Uh, hi," Stuart said and forced a grin out of habit. He tended to get nervous when he was out of his comfort zone and wasn't sure what to say. There was little doubt that this situation was definitely outside of his comfort zone.

The man on the throne laughed. "Hi, yourself," he said. "Come closer and enjoy the fire."

Stuart started to take a step, but a glance in the direction of the alligators caused him to rethink the invitation. "Uh..." he stammered.

The man on the throne nodded and a not so gentle nudge from Bluto started Stuart moving. The gators eyed him the entire time and he could have sworn the one closest to him licked his lips.

"Who are you?"

"St--Stuart. Uh, Hanson," he stammered. "Stuart Hanson."

"Well, Stuart Hanson, I'd say you made a wrong turn somewhere, wouldn't you agree?"

"Uh, yeah," he answered, trying hard not to shake. "Big wrong turn."

"And now you're here.

"It would appear so."

"I see," the man on the throne said. "And what do you think of my little kingdom here under the Mighty Metro?"

"It's... uh," Stuart stammered, searching for the right thing to say. "It's nice. I love what you've done with the place."

The man on the throne looked at him with serious eyes. He leaned forward and Stuart gulped audibly. Then the man smiled, which only served to terrify Stuart more. "Thank you. I'm rather proud of it myself," the man said. "If you had seen this place when I'd gotten here, oh, there was no organization. It was pure chaos. I hate chaos."

"I can... understand that," Stuart lied. "Chaos is... bad."

"Yes. It is."

"So, uh...?"

"Oh," the man said as if remembering an important detail. "Where are my manners? I forgot to introduce myself. I am called Maximus, Mr. Hanson. Welcome to my domain. All you see around you belongs to me."

"Nice to meet ya, Max," Stuart said, making every effort to remain aloof and keep the fact that he was scared to death under wraps.

"Walk with us," Maximus said and Stuart felt the rope tying his hands together loosen as Bluto untied his hands.

Maximus stood and walked toward another curved archway along the far wall behind his throne. The alligators obediently fell into step with him before the chains tightened. Stuart wouldn't have thought it possible, but they were obviously well trained and obedient. They were not subservient creatures by nature so they either feared or respected the man holding their chains in one hand and a staff in the other. Stuart understood because Maximus scared the hell out of him, maybe even more than the alligators he controlled. He decided the best thing he could do was stay on Maximus' good side as long as possible so he did as instructed and followed him through the arch. When he came out the other side he could have sworn he'd traveled back in time.

Stuart gasped. His mind couldn't easily process what he saw in front of him.

It was an arena. The main floor was circular, with the center was open and rows of seats encircling it. They stepped to the edge and looked over the wait high wall at the arena ten feet below.

"Incredible, is it not?" Maximus asked with a flourish.

"It is," Stuart had to admit. "I've never seen anything like it."

"This was once a bustling area of commerce, Stuart. May I call you Stuart?" he asked, but kept talking without waiting for a response. "This place was one of the old abandoned subway tunnels that had been boarded up decades ago as our beloved Metro City created new, more modern stations. Instead of filling them in, the city decided that it was simply easier and cheaper to board them up and forget about them. And now it is mine."

"What do you do here?"

"I'm so glad you asked," Maximus said with a smile. "I think a small demonstration is in order."

Stuart tensed. He had sensed the movement behind him before he felt it. A pair of hands, Bluto's he assumed, hit him hard in the back and pushed him forward. Gravity worked against him and he tipped over the wall and dropped ten feet to the arena floor.

Unlike the rest of the place, the floor of the arena was made of small four inch by four inch tiles that were holdovers from the time when this was a subway station. A thin coat of damp sand covered the floor, but not enough to absorb the impact of his landing.

Stuart pushed himself to his feet and looked up. Above him, Maximus was smiling.

"What the hell, dude?" Stuart shouted as anger replaced fear.

Maximus said nothing, but he did point to a spot behind him. Stuart turned to follow the madman's line of sight just in time to see a cage door ratchet open slowly. The tunnel was large enough for him to escape through, but it was also dark and had been closed with a gate. Something told him that Maximus wasn't showing him the way out. He was giving him a head's up.

"You might need this," Maximus called from above a second before a large stick with a knife attached to the end landed next to him. It was a homemade spear of some kind.

Stuart bent down and picked it up, never taking his eyes off the open cage door.

"Are you ready, Stuart?" Maximus called out.

"No!"

"Too bad," Maximus said. "Release him."

"Release who?" Stuart asked.

One of Maximus' giant pet alligators ran into the circle and roared.

"Never mind," Stuart said, wondering how he was going to get out of this alive.

•••

The Wraith watched from the shadows as the great beast finally made its way home. As with the previous tunnels, the mouth of this one was marked by a curved archway. Next to the arch was a ladder leading upward into a dark shaft. Deciding that recon was preferably to rushing in full bore, The Wraith switched on the night vision goggles in his cowl and climbed up the ladder. It was a tight squeeze, but after roughly ten feet he popped up in another tunnel almost identical to the one he had just left.

The tunnel was empty so The Wraith moved closer to the arch and looked out over what looked like an abandoned subway station. He knew that the city was littered with a series of outdated and unused subway stations. This must have been one of them.

"What's this?" he muttered as he turned off the night vision. Below was what could only be described as an arena. A man was in the circular space, his back against a wall. Across from him was a creature that The Wraith was all too familiar with. It was the same beast he had fought in the tunnels shortly after arriving. That meant there were at least two of the monsters roaming the sewers. Possibly more.

The beast's target was familiar as well. He was wearing the same clothes as the man he had seen vanish from the alley above. A crowd filled in around the edges of the arena, shouting and betting on the outcome of the cruel rodeo happening before them. Part of this group was made up of William Lassiter and his people as they were manhandled toward the wall to look down into the arena. The Wraith wondered if the floor occupied by the giant alligator was their final destination as well.

Another man stood apart from the masses. He was dressed far nicer than the other denizens of the deep he'd met. He wore a deep green cloak

ONE OF MAXIMUS' GIANT PET ALLIGATORS RAN INTO THE CIRCLE.

and carried a staff of some kind that looked to The Wraith like finely polished wood. That told The Wraith that this guy was either in charge or at the very least someone very important in this world.

That made him someone The Wraith would very much like to have a word with.

It wasn't an impossible drop from where he stood to the man's perch over the arena so The Wraith braced himself before pushing off and leaping into the air.

The dim light of the cavernous room made him all but invisible, except for the glowing yellow eyes that made up the chest plate of his uniform. All it took was one person to look up at just the right moment and see those blazing yellow eyes bearing down on them from above. Like a rumor, it spread through the throng quickly. By the time The Wraith landed in a crouch on the dais where the leader stood no one any longer paid attention to what was happening in the arena.

All eyes were on him.

"And just who are you supposed to be?" the leader asked in a way that made it sound like masked me with glowing yellow eyes dropped from the darkness above on a daily basis.

"That's funny," The Wraith said. "I was about to ask you the same thing."

"But I asked first. Manners?"

"Wraith," he said by way of introduction. He did not offer to shake hands.

"Really?" the leader said, tumbling the word around in his brain. "I like it. The name suits you. Wraith."

"And you are…?" The Wraith prodded. When the man smirked, but didn't answer, he added, "Manners?"

The leader laughed. "Touché, Mr. Wraith. I am called Maximus." He spread his arms to encompass the rag tag group who filled the stands of his makeshift arena. "To my loyal subjects, I am called Overlord."

"The Overlord of Under Town?" The Wraith asked with just a hint of sarcasm.

"Why are you here?" Maximus demanded, no longer interested in trading barbs.

"I'm looking for a man."

"Oh? And what man would that be?"

The Wraith pointed toward the man in the arena. "That one, actually," he said matter of fact. "I saw him get pinched from a dead end alley."

Maximus seemed amused. "So, naturally, you just followed him," he pointed to the man in the arena, "this stranger, into dangerous unknown territory?"

"It comes with the territory and the cape."

"Funny," Maximus said in a way that told The Wraith that he thought it was anything but. "And foolish."

The Wraith shrugged. "It seemed like a good idea at the time."

"I'll bet."

"So, why don't we dispense with the pleasantries and I'll collect that man, as well as the others you've taken and we'll be on our way," The Wraith offered. "No harm. No foul."

"I'm afraid not."

"I figured that would be your answer. Pity," The Wraith said and tossed a handful of small round pellets into the crowd. The pellets released a cloud of gas into the air that clung like fog to whomever it touched. Coughs and gags filled the air where there had been cheers and chants just moments earlier.

"Wait there!" The Wraith shouted to the man in the arena.

The man with his back to the wall nodded a response, but he looked as though he was frozen in place by fear. Having gone up against the big scaly critter that was waiting for a cue from his master to attack, The Wraith understood the sentiment. The alligator was quite terrifying, especially when it was bearing down on you.

The Wraith pulled a length of thin filament from his belt and anchored on end of it into the concrete wall with an explosive bolt designed for mountain climbing and hanging from the sides of buildings. Oddly enough, he never suspected it might come in handy beneath the streets of Metro City.

"Catch!" He tossed the filament to the man, who grabbed it. Despite the thinness of the wire, it was rated for three hundred pounds, possibly even more if he had to push its limits.

"Now, climb!" The Wraith shouted at the man just as he caught movement out of his peripheral vision. One of Maximus' guards was rushing toward him, swinging a metal pipe like a club.

"I-- I can't," the man in the arena shouted.

The Wraith ducked under the guard's swing and placed an elbow in his gut, which doubled him over. The Wraith twisted, stood, and brought the same elbow downward in a hard thrust that caught the man in the back of the head. A grunt was all the big guy could manage before he hit the floor.

The Wraith went back to the edge and looked down. The man in the arena was trying to climb, but wasn't having much luck. What he did have was a very large, very hungry alligator bearing down on him now that Maximus was too occupied with the chaos all around him to keep it in check.

William Lassiter and his people had used The Wraith's attack to their advantage as well. They had broken away from their captors and Lassiter was motioning the weaker of them, mainly the children away from the fighting. The others, Frank, Andrew, and their companions were fighting back. The Wraith felt a smile tug at his mouth. Helping people was what he did, but there was something so satisfying about watching people help themselves. He was proud of them.

"Lassiter!" The Wraith shouted. "I need you!"

He had just enough time to see Lassiter point and shout something in his general direction, but he wasn't able to make it out. When the man who called himself Maximus slammed into him he had figured out the man's warning cry.

Maximus wasn't a fighter by nature, The Wraith noted. He had no style and even less technique. His punches went wild and were so plainly telegraphed that a blind man could have seen them coming. What he did have on his side was surprise.

The Wraith had been so busy trying to save the man in the arena that he'd momentarily lost sight of Maximus. It was a tactical blunder, but an unavoidable one if he wanted to help the man he'd come down here to rescue.

Maximus swung out with the staff and caught The Wraith on the side of the head and for a second or two flashbulbs exploded behind his eyes. While his costumed enemy was disoriented, Maximus hit him with the staff again, knocking him against the wall. He reached out and grabbed The Wraith's leg and lifted, angling to push him into the arena.

The Wraith knew there was no way he could stop from going over the wall so he grabbed Maximus' cloak and held firm.

Together, The Wraith and Maximus tumbled over the edge and dropped into the pit below.

●●●

The Wraith tried to shake off the exploding stars that threatened to make his brain explode. He was sore all over, both from the fight and the fall, although he suspected the latter caused more injury than the former. He was lying flat on his stomach so he pushed himself up and spit a mixture of sand from the arena and blood from where he bite his lip onto the floor.

His first thought was to find the beast he knew was stalking the arena. He stared ahead and found it.

And froze.

There were two of them.

At first he thought the blow to the head had resulted in double vision, but he quickly realized that the second creature, the one he had followed from Lassiter's camp, had joined his brother in the arena.

The man he had been trying to help was still frantically trying to climb out, but his shoes could find no traction on the slick tiles that made up the edge of the arena walls. He couldn't see Maximus, which was both good and bad. Unless one of the beasties had turned on him and ate their master then he was still a problem that would have to be dealt with eventually.

"You okay?"

"Do I look okay?"

"What's your name?"

"St-- Stuart Hanson."

"Okay. Listen, Stuart Hanson, we're going to get you out of here, all right?"

Hanson nodded feverishly then shouted a warning.

The Wraith spun and saw nothing but teeth headed his way. He pushed Hanson one way and he went the other. They were barely out of the way when the gator slammed into the arena wall with such force that the abandoned station seemed to shudder under the impact. Several tiles snapped loose from the wall and broke as they hit the floor.

The Wraith shoulder rolled to safety and came up next to a long stick with a knife tied to one end. He scooped it up and held it in front of him. It was doubtful that such a small knife would fatally damage the alligator, if it could even pierce its thick, scaled hide. Still, a weapon was a weapon and it would at least get its attention much like a mosquito when it bites you.

But the alligators were smarter than he gave them credit. One of them came at him and the other went after Stuart.

"Climb!" The Wraith shouted, but the warning came too late.

The alligator snapped at him, but missed, instead hitting him broadside and scraping its scales across the man's midsection. Stuart Hanson screamed and fell to the floor. Blood trickled from a half dozen small cuts. It wasn't life threatening, but The Wraith bet they hurt like hell.

The beast was playing with its food.

"Hey! Over here!" The Wraith shouted and waved his arms just as he saw Lassiter and Andrew reach the edge above. "Pull him up!" he shouted and pointed toward Hanson, who had miraculously managed to hold onto the filament.

They set about their work while The Wraith tried to keep the gators occupied. They each stared at him, snarls escaping their snouts and he stood his ground, spear held out in front of his body in a defensive posture.

"Come and get it, boys," he said softly. All he had to do was buy Lassiter time to get Hanson out of the arena then he could follow suit and all of them could get out of the tunnels and back to the civilization above.

He took a step back, followed by another, and then another as the alligators approached. That's when The Wraith caught sight of Maximus. He was standing behind them, shouting order to them. The Wraith couldn't tell how the man had managed to control these wild animals, but somehow he was able.

The closest alligator snapped at him and The Wraith dodged then reared back and with all the force he could muster stabbed at the beast's next with the makeshift spear. The knife lodged between two scaled sections and stuck. The gator thrashed, more out of annoyance than pain from the look of it, but The Wraith held on tight to the handle until it snapped under the strain.

Now armed with only a short piece of wood, The Wraith took a couple steps back. Behind the beasts, he could see that Lassiter and his people had gotten Stuart Hanson free of the arena. Once he was safely away, The Wraith would focus on doing the same for himself.

He tossed the broken staff at the nearest animal and hit it in the face. The beast staggered back a step the lunged forward blindly, snagging his partner in the process. The second alligator roared as its friend's teeth dug in and it fought back.

That was all the diversion The Wraith needed.

He bolted for the opening with the caged door that had been rolled away. This was the entrance the alligators used to get inside the arena. Since he had followed one of them here and it made its way inside that meant that there was a way out through this side tunnel. All he had to do was find it while the future handbags fought amongst themselves.

He was almost to the opening when something hit him broadside.

Maximus! The Wraith realized. In all of the turmoil with the alligators he had forgotten about Maximus, but the self-proclaimed Overlord of the

Underworld had not forgotten about The Wraith.

The Wraith slammed into the wall and, off balance, toppled to the floor. Pools of water filled the uneven tunnel that led from the arena. It was cold and snapped him back to attention quickly. The Wraith swung a fist wildly and was rewarded by a pained grunt as it made contact with Maximus' jaw.

The overlord fell backward and gave the dread avenger all the time he needed to get back on his feet. "Your reign of terror has reached its end, Maximus," The Wraith said even as the Eyes of Judgement on his uniform's chest began to glow. "You dare to enslave these people and make them do your bidding? You should be ashamed of yourself."

The golden light of The Wraith's Judgement Stare washed over Maximus as if it were a warm embrace. The overlord's face went slack, his eyes wide as he relived every injustice he had committed against those he had perceived as weaker than he saw himself. He had thought them inferior, nothing more than cattle to be led around by the nose and to suffer and die at his command and for his own amusement. But now, bathed in the light of the Judgement Stare, Maximus' eyes were finally opened wide and he realized just what he had done.

"You have been judged, Maximus," The Wraith said softly as his enemy sank to his knees, sobbing. "The Eyes of Judgement have found you guilty."

"Yes," Maximus croaked. "I'm guilty."

The Wraith stood at the arch and stared into the arena. The alligators had finished their lovers quarrel and had refocused on the two humans that were closest to them. Whatever control Maximus had over them had obviously been severed, courtesy of the Judgement Stare, no doubt.

They started toward The Wraith, who tugged on the open gate. Gravity took over and slammed the gate closed with a loud *clang!* before the alligators could reach the tunnel entrance.

The Wraith stood mere inches from the alligators as they tried to get through the steel gate, but it held firm. Unless they learned how to climb the slick tile walls, which he doubted or else Maximus would have chosen another way to keep them in the arena instead of chasing the crowds in the stands, they weren't going anywhere. He would make sure to send animal control back down into the abandoned transit system to look for them. Maybe the zoo might find a good home for the animals.

"Time to go, Maximus," The Wraith said.

"Where are we going?" Maximus asked quietly, as though he was a little child terrified of monsters that lurked in the darkness under his bed.

"To the surface," The Wraith matter of fact as he grabbed the former overlord by his coat and pushed him forward to the exit.

"But I don't like the surface," Maximus whined.

"Too bad."

•••

The Wraith had never been so happy to see sunshine.

The sun was just starting to rise on the horizon that was hidden from view, but shafts of orange and yellow cut through the gaps between the buildings as Metro City prepared to start another busy day.

After they were free of the arena and he was certain that the alligators would not be able to escape and possibly hurt anyone else, The Wraith and Stuart Hanson made their way toward the surface. William Lassiter and a few of his friends accompanied them to make sure they didn't get lost along the way since they knew the sewer system far better than either of the newcomers did.

Once topside, The Wraith told Lassiter to meet him at this same spot that evening. He had a friend who would be willing to help them by donating some food and warm weather gear. It wasn't much, all things considered, but he would have Leena put something together to help them out. Perhaps she could even find a spot for William Lassiter somewhere in their business.

They said their good-byes and The Wraith placed an anonymous call to the police and left a message for Detective Rosa Perez to come to the alley. Stuart Hanson agreed to wait for the detective so he could explain things and turn Maximus over to the police. He also would inform them of the giant beasts that were lurking below.

The Wraith waited on a nearby roof until Perez and her partner Detective Sloan arrived. Once they had the situation in hand The Wraith headed home. He was exhausted.

•••

Paul Sanderson took a deep breath and smiled.

"Well this is a surprise," a familiar voice called from behind as Leena Patterson stepped out onto their balcony patio with a cup of espresso and a small plate of eggs and toast. Every morning she sat on the patio in her robe and bare feet before starting the day. She had once told him that breakfast was the only serene moment in her otherwise hectic work schedule.

He hated to interfere with her private time, but he had wanted to see her this morning before heading off to bed. He gave her a tired, but sincere smile. "A good surprise, I hope."

"Very much so," she said as she stepped up on her tiptoes and kissed him on the cheek. "Why are you still up?" There was a tinge of concern in her voice.

"After the night I had I felt like looking at the sky, that's all," he told her as they sat at the iron breakfast table.

Leena popped a bite of toast in her mouth. "Rough night?" she asked.

"You could say that," Paul said.

"Want to talk about it?"

"I'll tell you later," Paul said, leaning his head back against the chair and staring up into the cloudless blue skies over his beloved Metro City. It was going to be a beautiful day.

"Okay."

"Right now I just want to sit here and enjoy this," Paul said. "I spend so much time in the dark corners of the city that sometimes I forget just what it is I'm fighting for. Then I see this view and I remember so clearly why I love this place."

Leena watched as Paul slipped off to sleep on the patio. He looked so peaceful that she dared not wake him. Instead, she brought out a blanket from inside and covered him with it. She enjoyed her breakfast and stared out at the beautiful sky for the man she loved and dreamed of a day when their vision of a safe and peaceful Metro City would come true.

The End.

ESSAY - The Wraith "OVERLORD OF UNDER TOWN"

I've known Frank Dirscherl, creator of The Wraith for a number of years. What's weird is that he and I have never met face to face, but thanks to the beauty that is the internet we've talked quite a bit and I consider him a dear friend. In fact, we've also worked together before this anthology as well. The first book we were both part of was Airship 27's first volume of Lance Star: Sky Ranger and have since co-written a The Wraith novel called *Sanderson of Metro* for his Trinity Comics. I'd also enjoyed Frank's The Wraith novels and comics so I was pretty familiar with the character so it was a no-brainer when Frank asked if I would be interested in penning a Wraith tale for this Airship 27 collection. You should definitely search for Frank's novels, which are pretty easy to find in print and as ebooks. You'll be happy you did.

I write stories for a lot of anthologies and that means I generally finish one and start on the next one, sometimes the same day. That also means I don't always have weeks and weeks to prep and plot the story in the same way I might with a novel. At best I usually have a general idea and then I get started and see where things take me. This is an interesting way of writing that has worked for me, especially with short stories and novellas. I start with a general idea and start writing and see where the characters take me.

In this case, the character of Stuart Hanson kicked off this story, which originally did not go underground. The original plan was for him to stumble upon a villain's lair and for The Wraith to have to swoop in and save the day. It was an interesting idea, but somewhere along the way I decided to go down into the sewers. Also, not a bad place to build suspense thanks to tight dimly lit spaces that smell.

It wasn't until I wrote the word *alligator* that the story fully clicked for me.

From there it was just a matter of writing down everything The Wraith did. And boy, howdy, did he do a lot. My only regret is that I didn't get to spend more time with Maximus and that I had to resist the urge to called him *Maximus The Mad*, which wasn't easy.

In addition to my entry, "Overlord of Under Town," (funny aside - every time I wrote the word *overlord* I misspelled it as *overloard*. I have no idea why, but it was odd and I thought worth sharing) this anthology features three other stories written by some of the best authors that New

Pulp has to offer. I know we all appreciate that you've plunked down your hard-earned dollars to give this book a shot. I hope you've enjoyed visiting Metro City as much as I did.

Who knows, maybe, just maybe I'll get the chance to return to Metro City again. I'm fairly confident it would be an exciting trip.

•••

Bobby Nash is an award-winning author. He writes novels (*Sanderson of Metro, Snow, Evil Ways, Deadly Games!, Nightveil: Crisis at the Crossroads of Infinity*), comic books (*Edgar Rice Burroughs' At The Earth's Core, Domino Lady, Operation: Silver Moon*), short fiction (*Mama Tried, Domino Lady, Yours Truly Johnny Dollar, The Avenger*), and the odd short screenplay (*Starship Farragut "Conspiracy of Innocence, Hospital Ship Marie Curie "Under Fire"*). Bobby is a member of the International Association of Media Tie-in Writers and International Thriller Writers. He occasionally appears in movies and TV shows, usually standing behind your favorite actor and sometimes they let him act. Recently, he was seen in Creepshow, Joe Stryker, Doom Patrol, The Outsider, Ozark, Lodge 49, Slutty Teenage Bounty Hunters, and more. He also draws from time to time.

He was named Best Author in the 2013 Pulp Ark Awards. Rick Ruby, a character co-created by Bobby & Sean Taylor also snagged Best New Pulp Character of 2013. Bobby has been nominated for the 2014 New Pulp Awards and Pulp Factory Awards for his work. Bobby's novel, *Alexandra Holzer's Ghost Gal: The Wild Hunt* won a Paranormal Literary Award in the 2015 Paranormal Awards. The Bobby Nash penned episode of Starship Farragut "Conspiracy of Innocence" won the Silver Award in the 2015 DC Film Festival. Bobby's novel, *Snow Drive* was nominated for Best Novel in the 2018 Pulp Factory Awards. Bobby's story in The Ruby Files Vol. 2 "Takedown" won the 2018 Pulp Factory Award for Best Short Story.

For more information on Bobby Nash please visit him at www.bobbynash.com, www.ben-books.com, and across social media.

The Warm Rush of Chilled Blood
Greg Gick

"Hey, Pike?"

"Yeah?"

"We got a problem."

Smooth and slickly handsome in a callous way, the man named Pike McLeod glanced toward the lanky African-American and frowned. It was two-thirty in the morning, and the illegal rave was just warming up.

Pike McLeod was one of the fastest rising independent drug dealers in Metro City, an overflowing urban crock pot of crime and corruption. Jake Coser served as his first lieutenant and "best friend." That meant that McLeod wouldn't hesitate to kill him if he screwed up, he'd just feel sorry about it afterwards.

McLeod specialized in the servicing of a very exclusive set—the young, hot, and too-rich-for-their-own-good collection of yuppie businessmen, bikini models, and rising political stars known in the best circles as the Beautiful People. Metro City's Best and Brightest; the Crème de la Crème, the Goldest of the Gold—but Pike McLeod knew them for what they really were. Shallow, self-seeking wastrels without a thought for anything but booze, designer drugs, and casual sex; pretty but vacant shells gyrating wildly across the dance floor below, lost in a drug-fused bacchanalia of Ecstasy and Keratin. It amused the hell out of him.

But it was those same rich losers who were keeping McLeod in his fancy uptown condo and bought his custom-made Harley. So at Coser's words, the young rave host's eyes narrowed.

"What problem?" he snapped. "Couple guys picking a fight? Get Garcia and throw 'em out. You know the drill."

Coser licked dry lips. "No...no, it ain't nothing like that, Pike."

McLeod regarded his lieutenant. Coser wasn't looking too good. Matter of fact, he was downright pale. "Then what is it?"

Coser took a deep breath. "There's a guy on the floor. A *weird* guy."

"You mean like a perv or something?"

"Yes. No. I don't know. Pike, I—"

"Dammit, Jake, stop beating around the bush and *tell me what's going on!*"

Coser shuddered. "He's—he's giving out drugs on the floor, Boss," he panted at last. "For *free.*"

Pike McLeod let out a yowl that could be heard over the thundering sound system. "*What?!*"

Jake Coser threw up his hands. "I swear, Pike! How he got in, I dunno! Garcia says he didn't come through the door…"

McLeod wheeled upon his lieutenant. "Shut up! Where is this punk? What outfit's he with? Blackie's? If that jackass thinks he's gonna cut into my territory, I'll—"

"Pike—Pike, I—I don't think he's *with* anybody. He's—look, you just gotta see him for yourself. He's…" Coser shook his head. "He's *freaky*, man. Your eyes…they just kinda want to slide right off him. It ain't right. I—"

"Don't give me that bull!" McLeod's face was a crimson beet. "A punk's a punk! Now point this creep out, and you and Garcia meet me in the alley in five minutes!" A long finger jabbed out over the crowd. "Now, *where?*"

"Near—near the back of the warehouse, Boss. You can't miss him. Looks like a damned stick figure. I—"

"Outside!" McLeod roared, and his lieutenant retreated as fast as he could. For McLeod's part, he grabbed the rungs of the nearest ladder and started climbing down to the dance floor.

●●●

Mesmerized as they were by strobe light and bass system, the dancers paid the drug dealer no attention as he shoved his way rudely through them. As he moved, McLeod pushed his hand into his jacket; as always, the reassuring hard butt of the Glock 9mm brushed his fingertips.

There. That has to be him, the tall guy, shadowed away in that obscure corner; surveying the dance floor with a look of amused disdain. He…

Good Lord.

Good Lord.

Coser wasn't kidding. The guy is a freak.

Stick Figure towered over everyone else in the room; a seven-footer if he was an inch. And he was thin--not slender, not svelte but *thin*. Like a pencil sharpened too many times is thin, like a straw flattened beneath the wheels of a bulldozer is thin. Clad in a simple trench coat, he resembled nothing so much as a broomstick come to eerie life. Stick Figure's head was bald and smooth as a baby's bottom. But the skin—it seemed too stretched out over his scalp, and appeared as brittle as ancient parchment. And it was *white*: not the mottled pink of a Caucasian, but a sickly shade of decaying porcelain.

What is with this freak?

Pike McLeod couldn't keep his eyes on the stranger long enough to decide. Even as he stared, it seemed like his vision kept trying to *slide* off the figure; as if his eyes didn't *want* to get a good look.

The hell?

Stick Figure's own eyes were hidden behind a pair of wrap-around sunglasses. McLeod could almost feel the intensity of the stare behind those black lenses. For his part, if Stick Figure had noticed the dealer, he gave no sign. He seemed far more interested in peering intently across the dance floor; emaciated frame bent forward, thin neck craning outward like a predator stalking its prey. For some reason McLeod had the peculiar sensation the stranger was actually *willing* someone to leave the crowd and approach him.

She did.

Slowly, a girl on the edge of the revelers left her place and walked toward him, blinking, though whether from the drugs she had already imbibed or from the oddness of Stick Figure McLeod could not tell. The girl was definitely a hottie: red-haired, leggy and buxom, clad in sheer nylons and a black bikini top that left little to the imagination. She stared up wide-eyed at Stick Figure, who looked back at her with a sinister expression.

Like a cobra, McLeod thought.

Then he spoke.

"You seem the sort always searching for new experiences, my dear. Would you like to sample my wares?" The voice was soft, so sibilant as to be almost a whisper, yet carrying easily even above the rave's racket.

The girl blinked again. "Maybe," she said slowly, as she stared into the black lenses of Stick Figure's glasses. "What have you got?"

Stick Figure reached out a hand…and with a flick of his wrist a small plastic packet seemed to materialize between long, tapering fingers. In the glitter of the strobes, McLeod could make out the fine grains of a purple-tinted powder within.

"I have *Ophidium*," Stick Figure hissed fiercely. "And I assure you, it is not like anything you have ever experienced before. A source of euphoria the kings of ancient Atlantis reveled in, knew of its strength in the years before the barbarian conquered its hallowed halls…but today, it shall be yours. One taste and your life shall change forever. All you have to do is take it."

The girl stared at the packet, which the stranger was shifting from hand to hand. "H-How much?" she asked at last.

"Free."

"Free?" For the first time a sign of true consciousness glinted in her eyes. "Only the first one is ever free."

Stick Figure chuckled. "Not with Ophidium. The first sample is free, as is the second, and the third—and all that come after. As much Ophidium as you wish, whenever you wish. All you have to do is ask. Here. Take it." The girl seemed hypnotized at the sight of the glistening purple powder. *"Take it."*

Almost involuntarily, the girl's fingers curled across the plastic. "Now go," said Stick Figure, and stepped away. "Take and use freely. When you require more, return here and I shall give it to you."

Without another word the girl turned and moved back into the crowd. She did not look back.

And suddenly, Pike McLeod remembered what he had come for. God, for a moment it seemed like he couldn't even think. But now, thrusting a hand beneath his jacket, he stepped up behind Stick Figure and jammed the Glock into the small of the freak's back. "Don't move."

The colorless lenses of the sunglasses half-turned. They gazed down at the barrel as if curious but not particularly surprised. "Ah. And you are Mr. McLeod, I take it." The voice was casual and calm.

"Damn straight, freak. You know me?"

"Of course. I have been observing your organization for some time."

"Really. Then let's take a walk, dude. Through that door there."

Stick Figure shrugged, disinterested. "As you wish."

They crossed through a deactivated fire door into a dank, abandoned alleyway behind the warehouse. Stick Figure nearly had to bend double to slip beneath the door frame. McLeod herded him through and made certain the door was closed behind them.

Coser was waiting for them. So was Garcia, a tough-looking illegal immigrant who had once shot a DEA agent between the eyes. They stepped in behind McLeod as he prodded the stranger to the far wall. "Okay, punk, turn around. Before I put a bullet into your pasty white face, I want to know who you are and who you're working for."

Stick Figure obeyed, to regard his captor with an amused tic upon his lip-less mouth. McLeod felt another involuntary shudder. And his eyes were beginning to hurt again. "Well? Speak up, dammit."

"I work for myself, Pike McLeod. As for my name, you may call me... Coyle. Yes, Mr. Coyle. That shall be sufficient." A slight hissing laugh emitted from between his lips, as if the weirdo was enjoying some private joke.

McLeod growled deep in his throat. "Okay, *Coyle*. What the hell are you trying to pass around on my turf?"

"Did you not hear me?" Once again from out of nowhere a packet of purple powder slid into between his fingers. "*Ophidium.*"

"And just what the hell is that?"

Coyle gave a thin smile. "Not any new *designer drug*, I assure you. It is old; far older than anything you could ever imagine. And powerful. Yes, *very* powerful." He paused, but McLeod thrust the Glock further into his gut. "Please. I just want to show you."

Carefully Coyle tore the bag open, gently spilling its violet contents into the palm of his white hand and raised it to the dealer's face. McLeod waved it away. "Skip it. I don't do drugs myself."

Mr. Coyle chuckled. "Unsurprising. One cannot run a profitable business when one's brain is fried half the time, can one? Still, I did make the offer. Don't you think it's impolite of you not to at least accept?"

With a sudden blast of cool breath he blew a portion of the powder straight into McLeod's face.

Automatically, the dealer jerked back, but he could not help but suck in a small amount of the violet cloud that powdered into his face. "Whoa, man!" he gasped as the Ophidium mist swirled into his lungs.

And then, "Whoa. Maaaan….."

The Glock felt limp in Pike McLeod's hand. His knees felt watery. He felt *soooo* good.

He…he was in Nirvana, man.

And everything was Wonder.

●●●

"He got Pike!" Snarling, Coser and Garcia leapt to their boss's defense, fingers tightening on the triggers of their guns. But Coyle was already in motion. Before either flunky could take aim the gangly stranger had rounded on them, whipping his sunglasses off. Neither man could help but look directly into his eyes.

They were…unlike anything either thug had ever seen. So bright as to be almost luminous against the paleness of that sickly porcelain skin. Glittering green, with an intensity that reached out and stopped them in their tracks. The dark pupils—for a moment they were vertical, not round—bored deep into them with a fire that seemed to char their very souls.

As with their boss, their weapons became limp in their hands. All they could do was keep looking deeply into those eyes.

Mr. Coyle spoke. "Remain still while I deal with your former master." He turned back toward McLeod, who was leaning back against the alley wall; his mind clearly floating in an endless ocean of ecstasy. As Coser and Garcia watched, Coyle slowly began to swing his jaws open. But the jaws *continued* to expand—and expand, and expand, stretching out above and beyond the length of any human mouth. For a moment that gaping maw hovered over the tender flesh of Pike McLeod's neck. Then with a sickening *snap* they came together again.

The body of the drug dealer fell limp upon the asphalt, utterly lifeless. The living stick figure stepped back, jaws clamping back to normal. He glanced toward Coser and Garcia, who were still standing staring empty-eyed at their new boss. "Both of you. Go within and prepare to distribute my special wares. I shall deal with the remains of this carrion."

Without a word the two thugs twisted about and marched back toward the rave. Coyle gave a satisfied hiss. "You two are fortunate indeed. The Conjunction of Draco begins, and the original rulers of this world return. This city shall be the nesting ground of a new race, and you shall be instrumental in its rebirth.

"The Children of Yig shall rise again!"

●●●

"Good morning. Mr. Latham!"

Emerging from his private elevator immaculately clad in a conservative Armani suit, industrialist Robert Latham smiled at his secretary with regal but aloof magnanimity. Like a king might acknowledge a loyal peasant. Indeed, but wasn't he a king, of a sort, within Metro City? His company was one of the most influential and powerful corporations in the country. His cancer institute was on the cutting edge of research against that dread disease. His city beautification projects had turned downtown Metro into one of the Top Ten most aesthetic urban areas on the East Coast. As a legitimate businessman, his success was the envy and admiration of all decent folk.

His international crime cartel was the envy of everyone else.

Robert Latham was no less than the secret ruler of one of the largest criminal empires in the country. The unquestioned master of an international drug, arms, and slavery ring. And he loved it. After all the years of misery as an unwanted foster child, all of the mistreatment and disrespect, he had pulled himself up by his own hands and made himself a king. King of the City, as he fashioned himself. Both lawfully and unlawfully. There was only one small fly in the ointment.

The Wraith.

Of all the foes Robert Latham had ever encountered, only The Wraith had survived to remain a thorn in his side. True, the caped nuisance had never been able to topple him—but the crime lord had vowed not to rest until his antagonist's head was stuffed and mounted above his fireplace. Then that self-righteous bastard could spend eternity staring lifelessly at the portraits of all the dictators Latham admired so much—Napoleon, Hitler, Stalin—and know he had fallen to the greatest of them all. Maybe he'd have him directly face his personally-presented portrait of Dubya. Now *that* would be a hoot.

But for now the industrialist had other matters to attend to. "Good morning, Charlie," Latham said as he entered his immaculate and ornately decorated office.

"Oh. Mr. Latham," Charlie Grieco, Latham's head lieutenant, said, swiftly slipping off the corner of his boss's desk, where he had been carelessly lounging reading the *Sentinel*. Watching his lackey's haste, Latham felt amusement. Once, Charlie might have been Latham himself. In his eyes Grieco possessed the same feral look, the same hungry yearning for power Latham himself once had. The only difference was that Latham had channeled that hunger into victory, while Grieco…just hungered. The cheap thug longed to snatch the stars from the sky but his reach was too small to snare them.

In the meantime, it was funny as hell to watch him try. Plucking the paper from his subordinate's hand, Latham slipped behind his immense mahogany desk and said, "All right, Charlie. Let's cut to the chase. What have you to report?"

"Not much," Grieco confessed, checking his iPad. "Not as far as The Wraith's concerned, anyway. Only reports are of him taking care of ordinary robberies and muggings."

Latham grunted. He could care less what his arch-nemesis did to the rank-and-file of Metro City's criminal element. "Anything else?"

Grieco glanced back down at his screen. "No reports of freaks like Crossfire or Aztekoth, if that's what you mean. Everything looks pretty normal…wait. Here's something. Minor league dealer named McLeod apparently dropped out of sight about a week ago."

"Pike McLeod?" Latham brought his fingers together. "Yes, I remember him. Smug little bastard. Thought finding a niche among the rich made him a player. Who did it?"

Grieco shook his head. "No details. But rumor is some new guy took over his territory."

"Name?"

"Doesn't say. Want me to find out?"

Latham thought a moment, then shrugged. "No. It doesn't really matter. In the end, all the dealers in town get their drugs from me whether they know it or not. Well, if that's all that's been happening, I think we can afford to relax a little. Looks like Metro City is finally calming down. I—"

His intercom buzzed. "Your nine o'clock is here, Mr. Latham."

"Thank you, Candace. Send him in."

Already the knob to his office door was turning. "Mr. Latham?" a sibilant voice hissed silkily. A long, talon-fingered hand reached out in friendly fashion. "I am the gentleman who contacted you last week about purchasing a few of your old factories. The name is Coyle."

•••

"So the offer is acceptable?" Coyle leaned forward sometime later. "You agree to the sale of the property in question?"

In spite of himself, Grieco winced. No doubt of it; Coyle was *weird*. A living stick figure way too tall for the door, yet moving with a strange sort of grace, a sort of cold and regal sliding motion without seeming to actually step anywhere. It made Grieco think of a King Cobra he had seen in the zoo once. For some reason he couldn't keep his eyes straight on the man. Almost like this vision was being forcibly averted.

If Latham saw anything weird, he gave no sign. Instead he leaned back expansively in his chair and nodded. "Very acceptable. My attorneys can draw up the necessary papers this afternoon. Frankly, I'll be glad to get rid of that old factory. Since I moved production to Mexico it's been nothing but a tax burden."

"And I can take possession immediately?"

"Provided I receive the funds just as swiftly."

"Of course. In fact, I can provide you with a certified check for the agreed amount right now. One moment." A checkbook was produced, and long, tapered fingers manipulated a pen with a slithery grace.

Latham watched on, unblinking. "If I may, Mr. Coyle…"

"Yes?"

"This start-up of yours…"

"Valusian Enterprises."

"Yes, *Valusian*. Might I enquire to just what its products are?"

The black lenses of Coyle's sunglasses seemed to sparkle. "Pharmaceuticals."

Latham's eyebrow arched. "Pharmaceuticals. Really. May I ask just what kind?"

"Very old ones."

Latham folded his hands together. "I…see. Well, Mr. Coyle, for the record I happen to be involved in the making of *pharmaceuticals* myself. I hope for your sake your business does not interfere with mine."

Coyle's lips smiled tightly as he slid the check across the desk. "Don't worry, Mr. Latham. I assure you my product is *nothing* like yours. In fact, I do not even expect it to turn a profit." The smile grew wider and thinner. "Of *money*, at any rate."

For a moment, Latham regarded the tall figure silently, then smiled. "Well, that should be all, then. As I said, the papers should be ready for you to sign this afternoon. Here is my attorneys' card. I wish you luck in your future endeavors."

Coyle's head inclined slightly. "Thank you, Mr. Latham. And may I add, it has been a true pleasure doing business with the King of this fair city. It's always best to deal directly with the monarch, is it not? Cuts through so much read tape. Well, goodbye, Mr. Latham, and I am certain we shall renew our acquaintance very soon." And with that, the Stick Figure rose from his seat and exited the room.

•••

No sooner did he leave than Latham whipped out a cigar and ran his hand across his eyes, as if trying to wipe away something.

"Hell, Sir," Grieco gulped. "He practically told you he's going into competition with you."

"So he did." Latham shook his head a bit, trying to clear the somewhat blurry vision he had suddenly developed. "Well, let him. He won't be the first who thought he could just waltz into my city and take over. Let him fire up his little drug factories. Once he goes too far, I'll crush him like the stick-bug he is." The crime lord blinked several times.

That's better.

"Now beat it. I've got another appointment in five minutes and don't want you around."

Grieco left. Latham puffed upon his cigar thoughtfully a few times, then dismissed the mysterious Coyle from his mind. When Senator Bryan came in, he was greeted warmly. The good Senator was looking for certain houses that catered to his personal taste (children, preferably boys of eight or younger) and Latham was happy to provide. The crime lord was a dyed-in-the-wool Republican, but it never hurt to curry some favors on the other side of the aisle.

•••

"I WISH YOU LUCK IN YOUR FUTURE ENDEAVORS."

It was one o'clock in the morning, and Jack "Slasher" Grogan was bored. Very bored. Which meant someone was going to get hurt.

Jack Grogan was a thug, pure and simple. There was a reason he had been given the nickname "Slasher." The tempered steel blade with the shark-sharp teeth was never far from his hand. He reveled in its use. Be it a snarky hooker who didn't satisfy or a homeless bum he just felt like peeling up; with swift and bloody skill his knife danced across tender features leaving a gory jigsaw in its wake. Hell, just the other night he had carved into some little Korean grocery gook because she didn't hand over the till quick enough. So what if she had only been fifteen? It was fun.

But tonight—damn. Nothing to do. No good movies playing; the only thing on the tube that *American Idol* crap; and the newest GTA game not due out for another month. So here he was, parked in his car in a remote corner of Hyde Park with the lights off; smoking weed and waiting for someone to come along to provide some entertainment.

She came along soon enough. Tap-tap-tapping along in high heels and nylons, wearing a tight black jumpsuit that showed off every curve to fullest advantage. Red-haired, petite, with a fantastic pair of stems and a pair of the plumpest peaches Slasher had ever seen.

And high as a kite from the look of her. Eyes wide and dilated, and the expression on her face—it seemed almost euphoric.

Good.

That would make it that much harder for her to remember him. She was dancing as she tapped along, tight little body swaying to some tune heard only inside her head, oblivious to the world around her.

Lasciviously running his thumb over his blade, Slasher opened the car door and stepped out into the hot night. Time for some fun.

"Not tonight, Slasher. Not ever again."

The voice was totally unexpected and seemingly came from nowhere. Yet ubiquitous in the darkness, echoing off every tree and bush. A harsh voice, low and strong, almost a whisper—yet the sheer determination it held sent shivers down Grogan's spine. Slasher's eyes shot left and right, but could see no one in the gloom. Yet from out of the darkness the voice came again.

"Your time has come, Slasher."

The thug wheeled around, hand tight around his blade, but the speaker remained invisible. "Who said that? C'mon out!"

"An innocent girl is in the hospital with no face, Slasher," the voice was now behind—no, in front of—no—where was it coming from? "Did you enjoy that? Did carving up a mere child make you feel strong? You are not even worth being called a criminal. You are a coward, nothing more."

No one had ever called Slasher Grogan that—no one who didn't need extensive plastic surgery afterwards. Now he thrust his knife out openly, tip at the ready. "Call *me* a coward and hide in the dark, huh? Well, c'mon out, butthead, and let's see who the *real* man is!"

Bushes to Grogan's left crackled and a shadow stepped from the gloom. An immensely tall, broad shadow, brimming with power, muscles hard and tight beneath the blue, form-fitting costume. An ebony cape swirled about the feet and back of the awesome figure, even as his features were covered by a cowl of equal shade. That face gazed upon Slasher; the eyes a pair of stony white slits. Most eerie of all, as he threw his cape back, in the center of his chest there glowed two strange, illuminated slices of light that seemed to brighten even as they "stared" out at the thug.

Grogan's face froze. He recognized that figure instantly. Every punk in Metro did. All of them trembled at the sight of this, the self-appointed guardian of Metro City, the vigilante hunted by police and criminals alike, the so-called Dread Avenger of the Underworld.

"The Wraith!"

"Justice has come for you at last, Slasher Grogan!" With the speed of light a dark-gloved hand reached out for him.

And Slasher Grogan, thief, mutilator and would-be rapist, did the first sensible thing he had done all night. He turned with a yowl and fled for his life.

Slasher didn't have to look to know The Wraith was a mere few paces behind. He could practically feel the glove upon his shoulder; see those cold eyes blazing with a reckoning...

The girl!

Slasher had forgotten the girl! And there she was, tap-tap-tapping along in her drug-induced haze just steps away. If he could just reach her...

"Don't even think about it, Slasher!"

Slasher increased his speed.

Evidently the sound of the chase had managed to penetrate even the babe's psychedelic imaginings, and she started to turn to see what was behind her. Grogan pounced. Swiftly one arm caught about her neck; simultaneously the din glint of his beloved blade gleamed at an angle right above her carotid artery as he whipped her around to face his foe.

"I'll kill her, you son of a bitch! Swear to God, I'll kill her!"

The Wraith froze. But his eyes were those of a crouched tiger. "Release her."

"You crazy, man? You don't wanna see her die in the next ten seconds, you take your cape and leave. Or…" A pinprick of crimson appeared on the girl's alabaster skin.

The Wraith did not move. But, suddenly, the peculiar Eyes upon his torso seemed to light up. "You have just one chance, Grogan," the Dread Avenger whispered softly. "Tonight, one way or another, you face justice. Your decision alone shall decide whose justice it shall be."

Grogan snarled. "Ain't leaving? Then watch her bleed!"

"Your time has come, Slasher Grogan," The Wraith repeated. "Feel Emily Kahm's fear as you dug your blade into her face. Feel the terror and shame of all the women you attacked over the years. Feel the pain of all the men you have killed. Feel it—and know *their* justice!"

And then the Eyes upon the Dread Avenger's chest exploded into white-hot flame.

Here was the true power of The Wraith. The Judgment Stare. The ability to make any evildoer feel the pain he or she had ever inflicted upon their innocent victims. *All* of it.

Slasher Grogan couldn't tear his eyes away from the dreadful illumination. His blade clattered to the ground. "God! No!" he screamed. "Make it stop! Make it stop! I…I…"

"Feel the wrath of true justice, Grogan!"

The Judgment Stare poured from The Wraith's muscular form, sending waves of pain through Grogan's body. He screamed and collapsed backward onto the sidewalk, releasing his hostage and falling into unconsciousness.

●●●

The barest flicker of a smile crossed the granite face of the Dread Avenger. At last, justice was finally coming to one who long deserved it. And his innocent victim remained unharmed.

Ignoring the immobile thug, The Wraith stepped forward, leaning over to gently raise the girl to her feet. She wobbled unsteadily before him. "Are you all right, Mi…" he began.

Then the impossible happened.

He *felt*, rather than willed, the power of the Judgment Stare surge forth once again. The supernatural force sparked bright gold, even past the folds of the black cloak that now enveloped it. Before The Wraith could react, the girl's eyes grew ever wider, their black orbs seeming to take up all of her face. Her body, incredibly, slammed itself physically back, as if she had been suddenly struck by the full weight of a wrecking ball. The Eyes flared, lighting up the shadows surrounding the two, and the girl threw her hands over her face. Her mouth gaped open as her tongue lolled out, and she…

Hissed.

Then she collapsed, as dead to the world as her assailant.

The moment she did, the Eyes went dark. For a long moment, The Wraith remained frozen in place, utterly astonished.

Swiftly, he bent over the prone figures, felt their pulses. They were both alive. His hand dropped to his belt; snapped up the tiny radio he kept there. Within moments he had made contact with 911. "An ambulance is needed for two people near the corner of Kearnes and Acorn in Hyde Park," he barked. "A civilian and her assailant. Act swiftly." Without waiting for an answer, he switched off.

For a moment, he paused, eyes fixed upon the girl. A gauntlet reached again toward his belt; pulled a small black velvet container from a pouched holster. He opened it, removed a syringe. A needle gleamed like ice in the moonlight as he swiftly attached it. Kneeling beside the prone girl, he quickly plunged the needle into her arm and drew a small sample of blood. Moments later, syringe and needle were back within their pouch.

He could not tarry any longer, but he knew he was not done here.

Drawing his cape about him, The Wraith vanished into the blackness of the night.

●●●

"Mr. Sanderson! How wonderful to see you again! Are you here to see the Administrator?"

The eyes of the girl at the Welcome Desk lit up at the sight of the figure striding confidently into the lobby of Saint Lucia's Hospital. Trim and handsome, Paul Sanderson, one of the wealthiest men in Metro City and, until recent years, a recluse on the level of Howard Hughes, nodded with a dazzling smile that sent the young candy striper's pulse racing. "Good morning, Anita. No, I'm not here to visit Jack today. Rather, Miss Patterson and I"—at the words *Miss Patterson*, Anita looked daggers at the beautiful, supremely fit woman accompanying Sanderson—"thought we'd look in on that poor girl who had her face slashed the other day. Emily Kahm, I think her name is. As I understand it, her parents can barely afford the emergency room bill let alone any possible plastic surgery. I thought I might be able to offer them some financial help."

"Ohh—that's so sweet of you! Let me just look up her room—514. Fifth floor, turn left and straight down."

"Thank you."

His hand slipped into that of the woman beside him. Leena Patterson, Reference Librarian at the city library and Paul Sanderson's partner, smiled sweetly upon Anita as he started leading her away.

"I saw that look," Paul observed as he buzzed for the elevator.

"Well," Leena replied. "She was practically drooling all over you."

Paul shrugged. "Can I help it if I'm irresistible?"

Both laughed a moment as the elevator doors closed and the lift bean its trip upwards. "Well, as long as you had Anita back there panting over those big broad shoulders of yours, why didn't you ask about this other girl we're looking for? Afraid she'd faint from the sheer dominance of your overwhelming masculinity?"

Paul's face suddenly became very serious. "Because nothing about *her* made the news, Leena. Therefore, no reason Paul Sanderson should even know she exists. The only reason Emily rated a thirty-second soundbite was because of her age. Otherwise, no-one cares. The compassion of Metro City."

Leena sighed and nodded. It was true. Metro City was continually rated one of the three worst cities to live in America. No-one could keep track of all Metro City's victims. And no reason why wealthy socialite Paul Sanderson should even care.

Fortunately, Paul Sanderson—a.k.a. the cloaked vigilante known only as The Wraith—rarely listened to reason.

The elevator dinged and the doors opened. "Anyway, while I'm with the Kahms, I want you to see if you can find what room this girl's in. Don't ask a nurse. I want to keep this quiet."

"All right. What's her name again?"

"Bryce Greene. Hairdresser for a very trendy salon in Midtown. And a party girl, according to her record. Regular in every club in town, legal and illegal."

"She has a record?"

"Two arrests for public intoxication," Paul outlined. "One for possession of an illegal substance. Nothing major, but you don't party like she does without knowing where to get the hard stuff."

Leena took his arm. "Darling...there's something bothering you about this, isn't there? Something above and beyond her being just another rape victim."

Paul turned away, silent a moment. "The power of the Judgment Stare erupted from me without my mental command, Leena. That's never happened before, with me or my predecessor. *Ever.*"

Leena gave a start. Paul nodded.

"Even I don't know all the ins and outs of how the Judgment Stare works. The old man never had a chance to tell me...uhh...the original Sanderson that is. But we both know that it reflects the pain and suffering of a criminal's victims' right back at them. So a monster like Grogan literally feels the effects of every crime, every rape, every slashing he ever inflicted on others."

"It didn't work against Latham," Leena pointed out.

"No," agreed Paul. "It didn't. But it also has never activated itself without my mental command, either. When I faced Grogan, I had to will the Stare to power up, as per normal. But then, when I tried to help Greene—it activated solely upon its own initiative. And I felt...I felt..."

Leena gripped his arm. "What, Paul?"

Paul took a deep breath. "I felt a sense of such evil about her that it was as if the Stare *had* to react, even without my command. Something far, far more evil than a mere party girl with a drug habit should be."

Leena frowned. "Was that why you took the blood sample?" she asked in a low voice.

"Greene was clearly high on something when the Stare attacked her. But when Max and I analyzed the sample, all tests came up negative. We simply couldn't identify the drug in her system."

"And you think that had something to do with the Stare activating on its own?"

Paul shrugged. "I don't know. Anyway, see if you can find her room while I handle things with the Kahms. Regardless of what's going on, there's a little girl here who needs my help, and I'm going to make certain she gets it."

●●●

The room, as in all hospitals, smelt of cotton and antiseptic, the dull coloration of the off-white walls broken only by the green coverlet of the bed. No-one else had been in the room when Leena had found it, no concerned parents or siblings, no friends or co-workers. Bryce Greene may have been a party girl, but she was still very much alone. Leena found herself feeling sorry for her.

Leena had to admit the girl was beautiful. Small but exquisitely formed; lovely even wan and pale, lying prone in a hospital bed.

She's too young to waste her life with drugs and partying. Why do young people do this to themselves?

Bryce Greene lay still and unmoving, eyes closed, but Leena could tell it was not the stillness of sleep. The girl was comatose.

Paul then entered the room behind Leena. Without hesitation, he stood by the bedside and began examining Bryce's very feminine form, so intently Leena would have been annoyed if it had not been so clinical. Expertly he read over the hospital report clinging to the end of the bed and checked the girl's pulse. But it was not until he carefully pulled the left arm fully from its place beneath the sheet that he truly reacted.

"Leena. Have a look at this."

Her breath caught in her throat. "What in—?"

What she saw was astonishing. From the bottom of the shoulder almost to elbow, Bryce Greene's arm was covered with a deep blood-red rash like nothing she had ever seen. And it was clearly spreading. Tendrils of scarlet were starting to trail down the rest of the arm like obscene strings. At the shoulder itself, however, the skin was a sickly black-green. In addition to the ghastly colors, along the rash the skin seemed to be peeling and wrinkling as if shaping into some kind of scales.

"Eczema? A really, really bad case?" Leena asked, hoping more than anything else.

Paul remained silent. Gently he replaced the arm, moved to the other side of the bed, and repeated the process.

That limb, if anything, was even worse.

Gazing at Bryce's face, Leena was never sure how she knew, but she reached out and gently brushed back the wet hair from the comatose girl's brow. "Paul." The beginnings of the same sort of rash was starting to form upon the girl's forehead, even as the strange scaliness of skin was. "Darling—did the Stare do this?"

Paul looked grim. "I doubt it but I honestly don't know. According to the chart, there's no reason she should be comatose, nor is the rash responding to any medication. The doctors are baffled."

He lifted his head, and in the flash of the sunlight through the window, for just a second, Leena beheld the grim visage of The Wraith. "There's something wrong here," he said. "Something very wrong. I don't know what it is yet, but I intend to find out."

"So what do we do?"

Paul's eyes narrowed. "Max had word that a known raver, Pike McLeod, seemingly dropped off the face of the earth a few weeks ago. A big man has apparently taken over his patch. And he's heard rumors of some new drug being peddled. With Bryce here a known partygoer and drug user... there might be a connection. If so, I have a feeling Paul Sanderson and Leena Patterson might be on the illegal party scene sometime soon." They started to leave.

"But that's for later. For now, I've got to get some paperwork going for a little girl, and then, I think, lunch. Del Vecchio's all right for you, darling?"

•••

The room became quiet and still. Outside a cloud passed over the sun, closing off the bright yellow rays shining through the window and dousing the room in murk.

Bryce Greene's eyes popped open. In the gloom they seemed to shine a sinister, elemental emerald. A flicker of sun, and the pupils appeared, just for a moment, to take on a vertical slit like that of some venomous serpent. Slowly her dry lips parted, and her tongue, strangely long and thin, flicked out.

"Hsssssss."

•••

News traveled fast in a city like Metro. And as the weeks went by it was very soon indeed that word was on the street that an incredible new drug was ripe for the taking. In Metro's most prestigious banks and brokerage firms, its trendy cafes and high-class shops, its clubs and pubs and chat rooms, but always, always under the breath, the news was passed:

"Ophidium. The best high you can get, bar none. And for free."

At first no-one could believe it. But soon, those whom worshiped a certain lifestyle, discovered the rumors were all true. The stuff *was* free. No price, no cash transaction but however much Ophidium you wanted, whenever you wanted it. And the high—God, the high. An ambrosia river flowing through Heaven itself. Nothing—not Cocaine, not Heroin, not Ice, nothing else—could match it.

There was only one caveat. You could only get it in one place. A certain illegal rave-slash-drug party had been moved to a certain abandoned factory near the waterfront from its previous location. Under new management, the rumor was. But no one could deny it was better than it had ever been. The lights, the beat, the sex! It was like the drug took it all and then increased the sensations to their maximum effect. The Harmonic Convergence had nothing on Ophidium.

Best of all, they kept to the right class. Only the young, the rich, the powerful, were allowed into the rave. You did have to pay to get in, and they made sure the ticket was pricey enough to keep out the bums and street druggies. That was as it should be. Ophidium was simply too cool for the Little People.

•••

In the darkness of the office he had appropriated for himself, Coyle adored and worshiped his god in gratitude. Soon all would be in readiness. The Children would be born anew.

The king of this city had been as good as his word. Within hours of their meeting, the property he had bargained for was in his hands. He had to admit the efficiency of Latham's operation. The check had cleared faster than he had ever seen. The facilities had proven more than adequate to his purpose as well. In one section of the building, the Ophidium itself was produced. In another, things were being set up even now for the Raves, as they were called.

Both projects required more assistance than simply Coser and Garcia, of course. For the Raves, the floor had to be cleaned and prepared; walls had to be re-painted, old equipment moved out and the proper paraphernalia purchased and moved in. Many hands were needed for those tasks. Fortunately, Coser and Garcia had plenty of...*acquaintances*... whose sudden disappearance would not raise improper eyebrows. A few calls, a deep stare into eyes; an introduction to the wonders of Ophidium... and a plethora of new willing helpers were now available. That was well and good.

But despite the length of time it took, all the Ophidium was concocted by Coyle, with the help only of Coser and Garcia, alone. Ophidium was not a drug that lent itself to the ease of mass production. Several of its ingredients were extremely rare and fragile, requiring personal attention. The leaves of the nearly-extinct black lotus, for example, or the seeds of a little-known Tibetan flower that only bloomed beneath the light of a full moon. There was also the necessity of copious amounts of a certain viscous red fluid, of which Pike McLeod had graciously offered the first batch. Coyle was pleased. Everything was proceeding according to plan. So he prostrated himself in obedience to the great Yig, who he thought—

COYLE ADORED AND WORSHIPED HIS GOD IN GRATITUDE.

nay knew—must be looking down with favor upon his servant.

His reverie was soon interrupted. A rap on the door. "Master?"

Coyle sighed, but rose. "Enter."

In the light of the doorway, the silhouette of Coser stood black and cold. Even in the dim lighting, Coyle could see the change overtaking the man. The Ophidium was doing its work. That pleased him.

"Yes?"

"All is in readiness for tonight's function."

"Excellent. Tonight's show shall be the last. This very evening the call shall go out, and the new children will be summoned."

"Yes, Master. And the King of the City?"

"At my word, not sooner. The schedule must be adhered to. The Conjunction of Draco is very brief, and the ritual very precise."

"Yes, Master."

Coser—who was no longer really Coser—withdrew, closing the door behind him. The inhumanly tall, stick-like form of Coyle sighed deeply, suddenly feeling very weary.

Curse this city and its primitive inhabitants! Curse this world and the primates who have stolen it! But soon, very soon, the Cure will begin. And it will begin here.

Coyle slipped off the dark glasses that obscured his face. In the deep-set sockets of his eyes, two vertical slits, the eyes of a reptile, peered from the inky blackness. Peering into a nearby mirror, they seemed to glow, those slits, with an eerie, sickly emerald light. His jaw dropped low, far lower than was possible for any human jaw, and between the long yellow fangs the stringy length of a slender, double-pointed tongue slipped out. And the air about him was filled with the sibilant slice of an icy voice. "*Hsssssss....*"

"Tonight, my Lord Yig" he promised, his jaw now re-aligned. "Tonight begins the last reign of the humans. Tonight your children shall be reborn and the serpent shall rule the garden again!"

•••

It was a dank, dark street along the waterfront, pocketed with potholes and soiled with litter and human waste. Most of the street lamps were out, and the few remaining barely cast enough light to make it worth the power. The ancient, rusting hulks of long-abandoned factories and storehouses were saturated with the stench of brine, seagull droppings and other less savory odors. The pickpockets and muggers, ubiquitous in most of the other neighborhoods in the city, avoided the area. There was nothing worth stealing. This was the domain of the lowest of the low: the hopeless winos and drug addicts, the bag people, those forgotten and ignored even by Metro's poorest. Not the sort of place you'd find a collection of imported Mercedes-Benzes, custom-designed Jaguars, and slick Lamborghinis parked along the street.

But even among these this vehicle stood out. A perfectly preserved imported 1930 Daimler Double-Six, smooth, silent, and classically beautiful, regally winding its way among the more modern cars in quiet disdain. Paul Sanderson was very proud of this car. It was a true antique, given his predecessor as a gift by a New York millionaire named Wentworth. It seemed his great-grandfather had been in much the same line of nocturnal activities as himself and the original Sanderson. Paul didn't know if that was true or not, but damn, he loved this ride.

He and Leena sat in the back seat, but were not dressed in their usual impeccable evening clothes that meant a fancy night on the town. Their current garments were stylish but were better suited for partying than a quiet dinner in a classy French restaurant. Leena looked luscious in a pair of tight black jeans and short blouse, strapless and revealing loads of creamy white decolletage. Paul himself wore a silk shirt and pants, but they showed off his hard musculature to its best advantage. The only person in the car who could be seen as dressing normally was the burly, leather-jacketed driver up front; gritty Irish features obscured by the basic workman's cap upon his head. This was Max Horton, former criminal and both the first—and the current—Wraith's aide-de-camp. His responsibility was to help keep the Dread Avenger's equipment in top condition and also to work the streets, keeping an ear open for any criminal enterprises that The Wraith might be interested in.

"Was it hard finding the place, Max?" Paul asked.

"Finding it? Nah," the stocky Irishman replied. "The problem was getting the tickets. Whoever this bloke is that's in charge is only letting the super-rich in. Nobody else. Took forever to convince his boys I just represented a nameless millionaire who wanted a piece of the action."

Paul nodded. "And forked over a pretty penny for them, too. Whatever's going on in there, it required a lot of money to keep the local police away. I should be contacting Harrison or even Sloan or Perez. Let them know about this place. But they're too busy with the Murchison murders uptown. And much of the rest of the police force I simply can't trust. All right, Max, there's the place. Pull up to the door and let us out. But stick to the neighborhood and wait for our call."

"This isn't a good neighborhood, to say the least," Leena pointed out.

Paul jerked his thumb at the expensive rides outside. "Our rave holders won't want to inconvenience the clientele. They've already canvassed the neighborhood and made sure everyone knows not to mess with the pretty cars. Max'll be fine."

"What about the suit, Chief?" Max inquired. "If it went crazy earlier than…"

"I'm not wearing the suit at the moment. It's here under the seat. When—or if—I need it, I'll summon you." Paul swung open the Daimler door, stepped out, and held out his hand toward his partner. "Coming, darling?"

The man at the door was partially obscured by the night, but he glanced at the tickets Paul held out and opened the door willingly enough. Paul and Leena entered a cacophony of light and sound and scent: the flash of neon and strobe, the pulsating pounding of electronic rock, the smell of sweat beneath the hot lights. All around the people gyrated in flowing motion, heedless to the two arrival in their midst.

Leena looked around. "What do we do?"

Paul shrugged. "We dance," he said.

So they did.

•••

Like his predecessor before him, the stick-figure called Coyle looked down upon his work and found it pleased him.

Beneath the mesmerizing noise-and-light show, the shallow, mindless wastrels of this city danced their lives away beneath the influence of his "new" drug. They had no comprehension how ancient it really was. Coyle had told Bryce Greene the truth when he said the purple powder had once been known to the monarchs of Old Atlantis. Yet it was older than even that hoary old kingdom.

They also had no comprehension just how much they were changing. It would not show upon the surface much, at first. But, little by little, the change was beginning. Undoubtedly there were many down there now and others still across the city, who had noticed their skin developing odd, scaly rashes. Neither painless nor itchy, just annoying. "A little aloe vera; that should take care of it," they would say.

Pathetic monkeys.

How soon now would they find their old lives erased and their new, greater, world beginning.

Coser and Garcia appeared by Coyle's side. Their master hissed in satisfaction at their appearance. Coser's face was green-black, the scales shining in the light of the strobes. Garcia's transformation was lesser, but the slits of his eyes were vertical now. "All is ready, Master," Coser said.

Coyle nodded. "Then it is time to arrange for our guest of honor. Garcia, claim him."

Garcia nodded. His tongue, long and with the slightest trace of a fork, slipped eagerly along his thinning lips. "I obey."

Coyle turned his attention back to the ravers. A frown creased his pasty-white face. "Coser." A long talon pointed. "That couple. Have they been here before?"

Coser looked, saw an intensely attractive man and woman, both incredibly fit, dancing. "Not to my knowledge, Master. Why?"

Coyle leaned forward, his frown furrowing deeper. "They clearly are not on Ophidium—or any other drug, for that matter. And the male—his aura. There is a power clinging to him…I do not like it." Long fingers tapped the rail as the eyes behind the sunglasses narrowed. "I would know more about this one. Come. I believe it is time this celebration's host met his clients."

•••

Ordinarily, Leena would be enjoying herself. She loved dancing, and loved teasing Paul by showing just how flexible she really was. As if he didn't know already. Paul got back at her shaking-and-baking by looking ridiculous doing the Funky Chicken and she kicked him playfully. But neither she, nor Paul, were really having any fun.

"Paul, look."

He nodded. "Rashes," was all he said.

Every other person dancing were showing the same sort of rashes that affected Bryce Greene—on arms and legs, hands and faces, down backs and covering tats. Some were worse than others. And each and every one were obviously high, lost in their own powdered worlds. Not one of the revelers paid her a smidgen of attention as she stared at many of them one at a time. It was like the drug itself was staring them in the face.

She could see Paul felt it, too. He missed nothing of his surroundings. Leena knew he was absorbing every detail of the converted factory floor surrounding them. "See that over there?" he jerked his head toward the far wall.

Leena looked. A small area along the back had been blocked off with a black curtain, a small rectangular area with three huge gorillas blocking the way—gorillas with as many rashes as the rest. Clearly no-one was to be allowed beyond. "What is it?"

"Don't know," Paul said. "Maybe something, maybe nothing. Just got my attention." He glanced upwards. Leena knew he was examining the skylight above. The Wraith appreciated skylights.

"Pardon me."

Turning, they now faced the tallest, most slender man they had ever seen. Clad in black and with eyes hidden behind a large pair of incongruous dark glasses. Unlike the rest of the people around him, including the African-American accompanying him, this one bore no rash upon his skin. Instead, his face and hands were a pasty white and his lips were thin, nearly nonexistent.

"I beg forgiveness for interrupting your dance, but I do not believe I have ever seen you before. The name is Coyle. I have the pleasure of hosting this little celebration. And you are?"

"Oh, just a couple people out looking for a good time," Paul replied airily. "Heard good things about this party. Especially the free gift. If you know what I mean."

Coyle smiled tightly. "Oh, I do, I do. Mr. Coser, please give our guests our complimentary...treat."

From his pocket, Coser drew a packet of purple powder. Paul blinked. "That's it?" he asked, feigning disappointment. "I was expecting something... more glamorous."

"The best things come in the plainest packages, to paraphrase a saying. I assure you, this little powder shall change you forever. Truly. Here. Take some." He dropped the packet into Paul's hand. "Try it. You shall not be disappointed."

Paul looked at the packet a moment, then dropped it casually into his own pocket. "Thanks."

Coyle looked perturbed. "You do not wish to try—?"

Paul smoothly indicated Leena and himself. "My girlfriend and I like to sample the goods in the privacy of our home. Really ups the bedroom factor, if you...umm...catch my drift."

Coyle's face remained impassive. "Yes, I believe I do. Well, please enjoy my little party. By all means, help yourself to the drinks at the bar. Regrettably, you have to pay for those." With that, he turned his back on the couple and stalked away. Coser followed closely behind.

"Paul..." began Leena.

"I know," said Paul. "Time to leave."

"Can we look in on Bryce? I want to see how she's doing."

"All right. But afterwards…our white-faced Mr. Coyle will be getting a visitor."

•••

Several yards away, Coyle paused and his lip-less face smiled coldly.

"Master?" Coser asked. "Did you learn what you needed to?"

"No. I still do not grasp the reasons behind that young man's inherent power. But he has the Ophidium now. It will bring him to our side, and then we shall understand." He turned to his servant. "Go to the altar and ensure everything is ready. Prepare to send out the Siren Call within the hour. The Conjunction of Draco must *not* be missed."

Coser bowed and left. Coyle leaned back against the wall, watching the dancers, musing to himself. Soon the King of the City would be here. Soon the proper sacrifice could be made and the Children of Yig would truly live again.

•••

Robert Latham was not having a good day. An arms shipment to Iraq had gone sour, a rival drug gang was causing problems with delivery in Mexico, and now this.

"And it's *free*?" he inquired, incredulous, glancing up from his desk over to his lieutenant.

Grieco shrugged. "That's what they say—as long as you're one of the Beautiful People. Joe Schmoe on the street can't get it. At all. Which is why it's so damn weird. But then everything about that Coyle guy was weird."

Latham growled deep in his throat. He had known Coyle was going to be trouble but not quite so soon—and not quite like this. "And the high's better than anything we've got?"

"So they say. Called Ophidium, apparently. Haven't been able to get a sample yet, but…"

Latham rose from his chair, stalked out of his office in a fury with Grieco in tow. How dare this freak named Coyle challenge him thus? How dare he interfere with the operations of the King of Metro City? True, the actual profits from Metro itself were infinitesimal, given the vastness of the rest of his criminal empire. But sometimes principles were more important than profits. To have someone—anyone—cut in on ones own turf was unforgivable. A price would have to be extracted.

"Then hit him," the crime lord snapped, punching the button summoning his private elevator. "Hit him hard. Tonight. Doesn't matter who you kill. Just make sure that pasty-faced freak learns a lesson."

The light above the door blinked signifying the car's arrival. Grieco grinned. Seeing a little blood spilled would do him good, Latham thought.

"Sure thing, Mr. Latham. Anything else?"

Latham tapped his foot impatiently, waiting for the doors to open. "Yes. Get as much of that Ophidium stuff as you can and give it to our lab boys. I want it tested and synthesized by the end of the week. If it's that good, I should be the one selling…"

With a *ding*, the doors no-one but Latham had ever passed through slid open. Three men—if they could still be called men—stood grinning. For their faces barely resembled anything that could be called human.

They were reptilian.

Greenish-black scales instead of skin, with vertical slits in their eyes instead of pupils. One flicked his tongue out; it was long and thin and seemed to have the beginnings of a fork. "Hello, Your Majesty," he said in a sibilant, hissing voice.

"The *hell*?" Already Grieco was drawing his gun. The first of the Snake-Faces shot out an arm like a piston. Blood spurt from Grieco's mouth as he fell back. Latham started to step back himself, but the other two were already moving. In a moment they had seized his arms and one slammed strangely long, almost talon-like fingers deep into a nerve upon his neck.

Latham was out like a light.

• • •

Grieco was attempting to rise to his feet, but the first kicked him solidly in the face. Grieco went down for the count. Latham was lying limp in the other two's arms. One of the Snake Men turned, nodded. Together the three carried the unconscious mob boss into the elevator. The doors closed behind them.

Charlie Grieco lay on the floor, watching but immobile.

• • •

Nothing seemed to have changed with the unfortunate Bryce Greene. The girl continued to lay in bed oblivious to the world around her, unvisited and apparently unwanted save by two people. Paul and Leena, who stood by her bed, looked sympathetically down at her. Paul had his valise with him. It contained his costume as The Wraith.

If anything, the rash upon her skin had spread, turning her lovely face into a black-green mass of scale-like wrinkles.

She almost looks like a snake, Leena thought. *Just like the others at the Rave. God.* "Nobody here but us..." she murmured sadly.

"Perhaps that's why she turned to parties and drugs," Paul said, echoing her sadness. "No-one in her life. After this is over, we'll see how, if in any way, we can help her. But until then…"

"Have you any idea what's going on?"

"None, save Coyle is obviously giving out a dangerous drug—and for some reason, only to the rich. I can't help feeling there's something more to this." He fingered the lock on the valise. "But one way or the other, I intend to find out. I—eh?" Paul cocked his ear. "Do you hear that?"

Leena listened—but wasn't certain. Without warning, there had come a…pulse…a vibrating in her ears. Not a *sound* as such, more an almost sub-audible…*something*…that seemed just beyond comprehension. It had come all at once; the room crackled with it, and yet did not.

Bryce Greene's eyes snapped open. Then she sat up in bed.

And *hissed.*

Bryce threw back the covers and lunged to her feet. Her pupils were a vertical scarlet and, as she opened her mouth, the canines and molars and bicuspids had metamorphasized into yellow fangs. "*Geeetttt outttt of my wayyyyyyyy…*" the creature that had once been a beautiful woman rasped in the most unearthly voice either had ever heard. "*I heeaaarrrr the sirrrrenn callllll annndd IIIII mussstttttt gooooooo…*" She swept out a scaly arm and knocked Leena to one side.

Paul was on her a moment later. He had no intention of harming Bryce, Leena knew, just holding her. Perhaps that's why she slipped out of his grasp so easily.

"*Beeee gonnnneeee, primattteeessssss. Your day is donnnnneeeeee…*"

And then she was gone, barging out the door. Down the halls, they could hear nurses screaming in terror.

"Stay here!" Paul roared, snatching up the valise and following.

"Paul! Be careful!"

But if he heard his partner's warning, Leena knew not. For the Dread Avenger, too, was already gone.

•••

It was the same all over the city. People everywhere complained of a strange, throbbing vibration just beyond their conscious hearing—but everyone could see the results. Across the city, in expensive brownstones and fashionable apartments, in chic boutiques and restaurants, a certain assortment of people—all young, all rich, all with a disfiguring rash— suddenly rose from their seats as if responding to some inaudible tocsin. They paid no attention to those around them, save to knock them out of the way. But each and every one began making their way as fast as they could toward a certain factory near the docks.

Hissing.

•••

"Laathaamm..."

It hurt to try to open his eyes. Latham cracked his orbs, saw everything spin, and slammed them shut again.

"*Wake up, Your Majesty.*"

The contents of the water glass splashed upon his face left the crime lord little choice. He sputtered, coughed, and managed to wheeze out: "Have you any idea who I am?" before his voice trailed off. He couldn't believe what he was seeing.

The freak named Coyle stood before him, dark glasses on, but now clad from head to foot in a scarlet robe with the oddest designs on them Latham had ever seen. They looked like something he had glimpsed in a book once before.

What are they—glyphs?

Two of the Snake-Faces were firmly holding both of his arms. He was standing on a dais with a black curtain around it, although now it had been drawn back to expose itself to a vast floor—some kind of factory. Probably the very same one he had sold to this pasty-faced fool not too long ago. And the floor was filled with dozens, if not hundreds, of other Snake-Faces, male and female—with more coming in by the moment.

Coyle smiled.

"Greetings, King of Metro City. As to your question, I indeed know who you are. That is why you are here this evening. But do you know who I am?"

Latham snorted contemptuously. "I know you're a freak who thinks he can come in and try to take a chunk out of my kingdom. Others have tried. All have failed."

"Oh, I want more than just a *chunk* out of your kingdom, Latham. I want

THE FREAK NAMED COYLE STOOD BEFORE HIM...

it all. I want everyone in it. These"—he waved a long-taloned hand toward the others—"will be just the first of my subjects…the reborn Children of Yig, Father of Serpents!"

"What the hell is that supposed to mean?"

Coyle chuckled. "Oh, Latham, Latham—you primates do amuse me. Sometimes. But for far too long you humans have envisioned yourself the lords of this planet. You have no idea. Have you any idea just how old Earth is, Latham? Over four billion years old. And you believe that somehow humanity was the only sentient race to walk upon it? No, you pathetic little monkey—a thousand times no. I represent one of the first races to rule this planet—ruled with an iron fist that your kind eventually tore from us. But we did not die. Our numbers are pathetically few, but through you they shall live again. My Ophidium just began the change; with the Conjunction of Draco, I shall make it permanent."

Coyle stood imperiously before continuing. "In the past, many humans opposed us. The Valusian King, the Northern Barbarian, the Puritan. Humans of such courage and valor even we had to admire it. It is almost sad to see what wastrels you have become. These half-turned beasts, prior to their transformation"—he waved upon his audience—"were the kind that are actually *admired* by your species. They make television programs about their lives. Isn't that pathetic? Wastrels living only for their appetites. *That* is what the best of your species has become, Latham."

"What are you talking about?" Latham spat.

"But I shall give them a new life and a new purpose," Coyle said, ignoring the mob boss. "They shall be the first of a new generation of my people. Then, disguised in their old identities, they shall seem to resume their lives, but this time will use their money and influence to help spread my Ophidium to others in power. Then, very soon, the entire structure of your government will be made up only of my people—and the reign of your kind shall finally come to an end!"

Latham struggled, to no avail. "What the hell are you?" he demanded.

"We have been known by many names, Latham. The Annunaki, the Nephilim. But to those humans who are even aware of us, we are known as the Serpent People!"

The pasty-white face seemed to shimmer. And Latham suddenly knew why his eyes were always so bothered when looking at the man. Coyle wasn't a *man* at all—the entire image had been some kind of illusion! Now in its place, the illusion shattered, the full-on head of a black-green cobra—hood and all—stared back at him; long forked tongue slipping menacingly over a scaly chin.

The voice was still sibilant, but now completely inhuman. "Do you see above?" Coyle waved toward the skylight. "You cannot see the stars due to the light of this damnable city, but above us the Constellation Draco takes on a very rare conjunction. A conjunction that will mystically allow my Ophidium to permanently change my children here into full-blooded Serpent Men in the service of Father Yig. But it requires something to completely fulfill it. The sacrifice of the King of the City where the spell is being held."

For the first time Latham became aware of the table—no, an *altar*—behind him. And the wicked-looking blade in Coyle's hand.

"Tie him down!" Coyle ordered. "The Conjunction shall only last a few seconds and cannot be missed!"

Despite his best struggles, Latham was forced down upon the cold stone table. Ropes were tied to his wrists, binding him to the table, then the two Serpent Men stepped down from the dais into the crowd.

"You really should feel honored, Latham," Coyle rasped. The blade was held high; metal edge glinting. "The timing must be exact. And it must be…"

•••

The sudden explosion of glass from above caused Coyle to jerk away to avoid the falling shards. "What?"

A black-and-blue shadow swirled down from above. Landing hard upon his feet upon the dais, a figure of power and strength crouched instantly into a fighting position. The Dread Avenger of the Underworld, The Wraith, stood ready, having overheard everything Coyle had said.

"*You fool!*" screamed Coyle. "*Your interference has caused me to miss the conjunction! The sacrifice would be in vain now!*"

The Wraith smiled grimly. "That was the idea."

Swiftly he threw back his cloak, exposing the glow of the Eyes of Judgment. He had no idea what would happen, if the Judgment Stare would respond as it always had or if he would lose control once more. But he had to risk it. Only the power of the Eyes could stop Coyle now.

Mentally, he willed its strength to come forth. For Coyle to feel his own evil, to be overtaken by the vileness of his crimes. For a moment, the Serpent Man flinched back. But then, slowly, he stepped forward.

"I know you. You're the human I felt such power from tonight. But it seems something is wrong, human. Whatever it is you are attempting, it does not work on such as I." His jaw began to drop.

For a split second The Wraith froze. Thus far, the only other person who had ever resisted the power of the Stare was Latham himself. How could this creature remain unaffected while the others like him were?

But Paul Sanderson was The Wraith—and The Wraith never quit. "Then I guess we do this the hard way," he said and lashed out a foot.

The boot caught Coyle directly in the gut. The Serpent Man, caught by surprise, staggered back, falling from the dais. As he did, the blade tumbled from his hand. The Wraith reached out, snagged it, and wheeled. In a second he had sliced Latham's bonds.

"Emergency exit over there," The Wraith spat through gritted teeth. "Hurry. I'll delay them."

Latham gasped. "You're going to fight them all?"

"You want to?"

Latham almost smiled. "No. I'll go. And, Wraith…"

For a dangerous second, The Wraith glanced back at his arch-nemesis.

Latham grimaced. "Do try not to get yourself killed. That privilege belongs to me and me alone."

The Dread Avenger of the Underworld almost laughed. "I'll try, Latham." And as the drug lord raced for the door, The Wraith leapt into the fray…

•••

The Serpent Men poured toward The Wraith. A sea of black-green scales and ivory fangs bursting forth, ready to rend their enemy to shreds.

"Get him, you fools! Get him!" Coyle hissed, seemingly dancing in place in his rage. Latham had already been forgotten. "Destroy him!"

Now that the ritual had been disrupted, the drug lord's usefulness was gone as far as the cobra-headed monster was concerned, The Wraith observed. All that mattered was The Wraith.

"Destroy him!" Coyle repeated.

The Wraith hit the floor running. In truth, he had no idea what he was about to do. How does one fight dozens of reptile creatures from the dawn of time? But if he did not, Coyle could still somehow unleash Ophidium onto the masses of the city, changing the rest of its inhabitants into his own evil image. That could not be allowed. But even as he tensed and hurtled himself into the crowd of slithering snake-men, only one question rang through his mind…

How do I stop them?

Fortunately, someone—or something—answered that for him.

The Judgment Stare exploded forth, more intense than any strobe above, piercing the eyes like hot iron nails and blinding all who saw. A wave of Serpent Men fell back, hissing in agony. In his own chest, The Wraith felt a sudden, overwhelming rush of power bursting forth without his command. The Judgment Stare was burning the half-human, half-reptilian creatures with its purity. The Serpent Men screamed. The Wraith screamed. The power *burned.*

The intensity of the Judgment Stare erupted again and again and again, sending the hybrid monsters to the floor. But for every one struck down there were two still clawing forward, groping for The Wraith, driven on by instinctive hatred drawn from their reptilian brains for the hairy primate who dared confront them.

The Dread Avenger could hear the hideous voice of Coyle still shouting from the altar. There, he knew, was his true foe. These...*creatures*...were that ancient monster's victims, though no less dangerous.

The Serpent Men were crawling over each other to get to him, ripping at his cape even as the Stare drove them back or into unconsciousness. There was only one thing to do. The Wraith yanked out his grappling hook and sent the line hurtling toward the ceiling. The sudden tautness of the cord told him he had snagged a brace. Pressing the retract button, he swiftly rose upward so none of the Serpent Men could follow. Once high enough he glared at Coyle, judged the distance between him and it, and flung himself through the air. Coyle cocked his cobra-like head before he could react further. Almost instantly, The Wraith was upon him.

"Get your filthy paws off me, primate! Your inferior race is through! The original masters of this planet return and your kind must be swept aside!"

"*Shut...up!*" The Wraith growled and sent a fist slamming into Coyle's snout.

The Eyes of Judgment, so wild when facing the half-human Serpent Men, faded instantly when confronted with Coyle. He still had the knife he had used to free Latham. Would subduing—or even killing—Coyle somehow return the Serpent Men back to their human form? He knew not. But he dared not allow this unholy creature to unleash his malicious drug on the rest of Metro! He struck the Serpent Man again and again—and yanked the knife free from its makeshift holster.

Coyle fought back. A long arm swept out, knocking The Wraith to the floor. The Dread Avenger was on his feet in an instant, ignoring the flow of blood coursing down from his nose and lips.

Before he could move, Coyle threw out his arms and tossed his head back, hissing. "*Oh, Great Yig! Help your loyal servant in his hour of need! This interloper dares strike against your new children in their most vulnerable hour! Strike him down and give glory to your name!*"

The Wraith darted forward. The blade was ready, poised to pierce the monster's heart.

And then it happened.

Coyle received an answer.

The Wraith couldn't be certain where the voice came from. It was just… *there*, low and deep. Ringing throughout the factory. Completely inhuman in its sheer malignancy.

"*NO.*"

At the sound of the word everyone—Coyle, the Serpent Men, even The Wraith—froze. In the few years since becoming taking over as the Dread Avenger, Paul Sanderson had encountered horrors beyond his comprehension. But he felt his very sanity freezing at the sound of that voice.

"*THE CONJUNCTION OF DRACO HAS PASSED. I DID NOT TASTE THE BLOOD OF A KING. AND YOU HAVE FAILED ME. I WITHDRAW MY FAVOR FROM YOU. I STRIKE THESE HYBRIDS FROM MY PRESENCE. SO AS THEY ARE NEITHER MEN NOR SERPENT MEN, SO SHALL THEY BE PERMANENTLY. AS SHALL YOU.*"

"*Nooooooo!*" screamed Coyle. "*Father Yig, no!*"

But the voice was implacable. "*I GO NOW. BUT FOR YOUR EARLIER SERVICE TO ME, ONE BOON I GIVE YOU: THE POWER TO CRUSH YOUR ENEMY BETWEEN YOUR COILS. IF YOU CAN.*"

And then it was gone.

Coyle howled in despair. The other Serpent Men followed suit. The Wraith, thrusting what had just occurred to the back of his mind, launched himself forward once again. He grappled with Coyle, knife flashing in the strobe lighting, as the victims of Ophidium began climbing the dais, yanking upon the vigilante's cape. The Wraith felt the power of the Judgment Stare rise again.

But the change had already begun.

The rest of the Serpent Men froze in place, seemingly unable to move. Their faces, caught somewhere between human and reptile, began to flow, reshaping themselves into a more ophidic shape, much like Coyle's true visage. Noses and mouths extended into blunt snouts, eyes enlarged and twisted around to the sides of their heads. *But*—even as their faces changes, so to did their bodies. To begin with, their forms shuddered, seeming to suddenly shrink in on themselves. And then The Wraith realized it—they *were* shrinking, becoming smaller in size with every passing second.

And there was still more. The Serpent Men's arms suddenly pressed hard against their torsos even as their legs followed into each other. As they did, their limbs seemed to *melt* into their bodies, being absorbed by the very flesh of chest and hip. The Serpent Men fell, unable to stay upon their no-longer existent feet. Their bodies wriggled as if they had no bones. Shoulders vanished as head and neck merged into one, torsos became tubular…and The Wraith was no longer looking at anything remotely resembling a human. He was looking at *snakes:* a hundred, two hundred or more ropy green-black serpents with wicked emerald eyes, flopping limply to the floor. Some drew their coiling bodies back as if in astonishment. Others gaped their wide mouths open and hissed coldly. But one and all twisted about, away from the dais and their former master, fleeing the lights above for the safety of darkness.

"My children!" gasped Coyle. "My children! No!" Then a shudder ripped across his body and he filled the air with a scream no human throat could possibly duplicate.

The Wraith jerked back in time to see the same metamorphosis overcome his foe. Coyle's body quivered, his limbs melted into his torso and his body elongated even more than it already was. His hooded cobra-head did not change shape, but strangely, the eyes were becoming duller. The cold, malignant intelligence, the evil sentience, was fading from them. But, unlike his brethren, the thing that had been the Serpent Man called Coyle was not shrinking overall in size. Rather he was lengthening, *growing,* becoming longer and thicker and more muscular than any python, any anaconda, on Earth had ever been. Before The Wraith's startled eyes, the serpent was becoming a giant.

A maw as wide as a hippo's opened fully. Fangs the length of a man's arm glinted in the strobe lighting. "*Maaannnnnn…*" the snake-creature spat out in his last intelligible words, "*You did thiiiissssss…*"

The monster wheeled upon The Dread Avenger, dull green eyes flashing one last time with hatred. The tree-trunk-sized body flexed and suddenly a massive coil was around The Wraith, pressing inward. The Wraith gasped as most of the air was squeezed from his lungs as the gigantic monster squeezed. He feared he was going to die, crushed in the coils of this hideous monster!

"*Hsssssss…*" The mighty hood, now the length of a glider's wings, spread out wide. The outrageous jaws began to lower. On the tips of the yellow fangs, The Wraith could just see the first drips of venom appearing. The last thing Coyle—or what was once known as Coyle—was going to do in his fading sentience was to kill The Wraith, he who had cost him everything. If the coils didn't get him, the poison would.

The Wraith pulled with everything he had. It took a herculean effort, but the Dread Avenger managed to force one arm and hand free. The arm and hand that still clung to the sacrificial knife that would have killed Latham just minutes before.

He knew this was his one and only chance. If he failed, it would be the end.

The gaping red maw was almost upon him now. The Wraith jerked his arm back, aimed, and threw. The knife shot through the air, up far into the scarlet mouth and throat of the creature.

There was a sick, fleshy thud.

The snake creature's head jerked back, jaws snapping shut. For a moment, the huge monster just stood there, a look in its dull eyes almost of surprise. Then, slowly, a slight dribble of crimson slipped down the green-black flesh of its jaws.

Then the body went spastic.

The Wraith rode the giant snake like a bucking bronco. The creature's mouth opened again, but this time the flow of blood was a river. The Wraith had aimed well. With the uncanny accuracy of a master knife thrower, his toss had penetrated the blade deep into the monster's brain.

For a moment, the coils about him loosened and The Wraith took the opportunity to act. With everything he had, he clambered out, barely managing to avoid being flattened by a heaving mound of torso. He fell to the floor, grunting with pain from his injuries, but the demon snake made no effort to seize him. It was too busy dying.

As The Wraith watched, the great body made a final spasmodic twist, then lay still. Slowly, The Wraith rose to his feet. He looked around. The rest of the serpents had scattered, crawling through holes and crevices, driven into hiding only the Lord knew where. As human beings, they were gone. The Wraith took a deep breath, shook his head to force his thoughts back into focus.

Painfully he reached for his in-cowl radio, which was used to contact his operatives, pressing at his temple to activate it. "Max. Come get me at once. Don't delay."

Switching off, he tossed his askew cape back over his shoulders. Then he marched for the nearest door. He did not look back.

•••

Charlie Grieco sat back in his master's Corinthian leather chair, feet propped upon the mahogany desk, grinning like a maniac and smoking one of Latham's prized Cuban cigars. How could this have worked out any better?

He had a hell of a headache, of course, but that was small price to pay. His first thought upon waking was to call the boys to get after Mr. Latham. But—he realized that was behavior borne of habit. He asked himself: what had Latham ever done for him except slap him around and think he was so much damn better than he?

An entire empire had just been dropped straight into his lap. And he intended to take it for all it was worth. So he did nothing but bask in the glory of this new empire. *His* empire!

Grieco heard the soft tread of footsteps outside the office. He smiled. Candace had gotten his text, after all. He and the secretary had been banging behind Latham's back for some months now. "C'mon in, honey. The new king has been waiting for you."

The door swung open. Looming in the frame, bruised, disheveled, but still very much alive was Robert Latham, who glared at his underling with a red-faced fury. "He is? Oh thank you…*darling.*"

Grieco leapt to his feet, his heart pounding furiously. "Mr. Latham, sir!"

Latham shut the door harshly behind him. "Yes, Charlie. The one you allowed to be kidnapped right under your nose."

Grieco's Cuban fell limply to the floor. Latham reached out a foot and crushed the lighted stogie beneath it.

"Be glad you didn't see what I saw, Charlie. I saw madness. A madness that almost killed me. And do you know who had to save me? Do you? *Him!*" The drug lord shook his head. "I'm going to be hard-pressed to forget what I saw tonight, Charlie. But believe me, I'm going to. It's going to be like it never happened. The only other solution is insanity—and I'm not going to go insane, Charlie. Not *me.*"

Grieco's mouth suddenly went dry, unable to reply.

"Unfortunately to do that, I need things just as they were before this fiasco. I need *you*, Charlie. Back as my right-hand man. So you get to live."

Grieco found words at last. "You—you're not going to kill me?"

Latham shook his head. "No. No, I'm not. I'm just going to make you sorry you were ever born. You see, Charlie, I might be going to forget this ever happened…but don't think I won't *remember*."

And then the beating began.

In earnest.

• • •

"Paul…they became…*snakes*?"

If it had been anyone but Paul telling her this, Leena Patterson would never have believed it. She didn't *want* to believe it. But, after Aztekoth, how could she not?

Paul was adamant. "I saw what I saw, Leena."

He sat upon a stool in the Lair, while Max hovered over him stitching up his left shoulder. Leena sat on chair nearby. Their butler, Jonathan Simpson, stood ubiquitously by with the necessary hot water and towels. What either he or Max thought of their master's unbelievable story could not be read from their faces.

Leena thought of Bryce and shuddered. *Whatever she did wrong, she deserved nothing like that. None of them did. Oh God, I thought I knew what I was getting in for when I chose to stay with Paul. But this…*

She felt a soft hand upon her shoulder. In spite of Max's protest, Paul had risen and, not heeding the pain, gathered Leena into his bruised and bloody arms, as Simpson quietly retreated.

For a long time they simply held one another. Silently Leena realized that, whatever had happened, there was no backing out now. She and Paul had chosen their path and, whatever strange and horrible form it might take, they had to travel down it. Together.

Moments lengthened before Paul resumed his seat. He gratefully accepted the glass of brandy the returned Simpson offered.

"I don't like these burns on your chest, Chief," Max grunted as he dabbed at the wound. "Sure you don't want me to call Doc Needham?"

"I'll live," Paul grimaced. "So much power was exploding from the Eyes of Judgment it couldn't help but burn even me."

Max applied gauze and bandages. "But what made the Judgment Stare go so bloody mad in the first place?"

"I think that the Stare's power is to connect with a criminal's own empathy; to make them feel the exact same pain and suffering of their victims. But for that to work, you have to *have* empathy, if only a shred. If they don't…if they lack all humanity itself…it would be like using the

Stare on a lifeless mannequin." Paul stood. "Look at Latham. He's the only man who's ever resisted the Judgment Stare up to now. That's because there's no empathy *in* him. He doesn't care about anything or anyone. He *can't*. He's human only in biological terms."

"But..." Max started.

"And then Coyle comes along," Paul continued. "A being who was never human...at all. The Judgment Stare *couldn't* affect him. It was never designed to do so."

Leena frowned. "That doesn't make sense. Why then did it go so wild on Bryce and the others? They, well, weren't human, either. Not really."

Paul ambled toward his butler, who held up a bathrobe and helped his master slip within. "Not quite, darling. They were in the *process* of becoming inhuman. The Ophidium was changing them, but they *had* been human, were still partially human beings. I think that's why the Stare went so berserk when confronted by them—I think that, somehow, it was trying to exorcise the Serpent Men influence from them. To try and turn them back into human beings again. Unfortunately, all it did was accelerate the change. Why I don't know."

"But how are they going to explain the body of a giant snake in a rave? Or how so many young and rich people just up and vanished?" Leena asked.

Paul shrugged. "I contacted Commissioner Harrison, told him the true story of what occurred. I doubt he believed me at first, but they've got the evidence to back my word up. That should convince the police." Absentmindedly, Paul ran his fingers across his chest. "Ever since becoming The Wraith...I've seen so many things I never would have believed in my old life as Michael Reeve. Now I'm learning the world is stranger than I ever imagined. Aztec warriors risen from the dead. Ancient Serpent People. Snake Gods. Even my predecessor never encountered anything like them. And—there's so much about the Eyes of Judgment I don't understand yet, so much the old man didn't tell me before his death. I have to know more. But I don't know how—or where—to go to find the answers I need."

"A vacation," Leena blurted out. "What we need is a vacation."

Paul flashed a tired smile. "Maybe soon, Leena, but...I'm not ready. There's still so much to do."

Leena sighed but knew better than to argue with the Dread Avenger of the Underworld. An argument like that would get her nowhere.

•••

Outside Sanderson House, in the well-kept gardens, a mouse, nose and whiskers twitching, scrambled out of its hiding place into the warmth of the sun-drenched courtyard, reveling in the pleasant heat. Chattering to itself, it looked for a good place to gnaw its teeth down, maybe find some tiny morsel for nourishment.

It never saw it coming.

The strike came seemingly from nowhere; a flash of black-green terror, yellow fangs driving deep into the rodent's furry body and injecting the venom. Within seconds, the mouse was dead.

Slithering out of the grass where it had been hiding, the emerald-eyed snake seemed to raise its body length up in triumph before devouring its dinner.

Ominously, it seemed to resound with a malicious sound of triumph: "Hsssssssssss…….."

The End

AFTERWORD

*P*laying with someone else's toys is always fun; but being *asked* to play with them by the owner is a great honor.

So you can imagine how I felt when Frank asked me to contribute a story for him for a Wraith anthology. To work with one of the best of the neo-pulp characters out there; a combination of modern storytelling, pulp heroics, and Silver Age superheroing! Wow!

Well, here's my small contribution to The Wraith mythos. I can only hope I returned Frank's toys in as good a condition as I borrowed them.

Thanks, Frank, for the sandbox.

•••

GREG GICK - is a devilishly handsome and dashing fellow; beloved of all mankind and friend to animals. His work can be found in Airship 27's Mars McCoy, Secret Agent X, and Men (and Women) of Mystery. He is creator of The Brown Recluse who is currently looking over his shoulder demanding the continuation of his adventures.

The Enemy Within
Erik Franklin

*I*t was a warm July night. Despite having removed his jacket and turning on the air conditioner to full blast, Detective Joel Wilcox was still sweating. He looked over at his partner, the bulky, slovenly Detective Rodney Burke, who was doing his best to show a calm facade. Burke's outward coolness was a lie, betrayed by the fact that his hand was gripping the steering wheel too tightly and his cigarette, which hung limply from his mouth, had gone out a couple of miles back.

Wilcox wiped his brow, knowing that the seasonal heat was not the only reason for his perspiration. It was fear. Ever since he woke up that morning, Wilcox had a sense of complete and utter dread as he went throughout his day. All Wilcox's senses were in a heightened state of alert as if he were a small animal that knew a predator was closing in for the kill. When he was working in the police station, every slam of a file cabinet or ringing phone caused him to leap from his seat. To him, they sounded like gunshots. Whenever he saw a shadow coming around a corner, he was certain they were coming to get him. The worst was when he and Burke were summoned to Commissioner George Harrison's office.

Thinking back on the meeting, Wilcox remembered Burke having an ominous look on his face as well. Although the two swore they would be able to keep their dark secret, each had privately wondered if the other would be able to keep their mouth shut. Last week Wilcox had a screaming match with Burke in the parking lot. Against their agreement, Burke had gone out and purchased that designer watch he had always coveted.

"What the hell were you thinking?" Wilcox remembered yelling at him.

"You know how long I've had my eye on this! And now that I can afford it, guess what, Joel? It's mine!" Burke bellowed back at him.

Grabbing his partner by the lapels, Wilcox quickly glanced around the parking lot and saw that they were alone. He growled at his partner, "We *can't* afford it, Burke! Don't you get it! *Nobody* is supposed to know that we have this kind of money!"

Wilcox remembered how Burke swiped his hand away, with a defiant glare on his face. "Will you relax for once in your life? Half the cops in this department are on Latham's payroll, and if it's not Latham, it's somebody else."

"Not everyone! What about goodie-goodies like Sloan and Perez? If you blab to them, they take it to Harrison and then we spend the rest of our life in prison... or worse! You know what happens to cops in prison!" Wilcox said, shaking with fury.

"Sloan? Perez? Are you kidding me?" Burke refuted. "Everyone knows that we outnumber the 'honest' cops on the force ten-to-one." Seeing that his partner was not comforted by his assurances, Burke placed a hand on Wilcox's shoulder. "I'll tell you what, if it'll make you feel better, I won't wear the watch while I'm working. Okay?"

Wilcox thought he was able to put that confrontation behind him, but it came flooding back as he followed Burke into Harrison's office. Had he found out? Whatever happened, Wilcox had determined that it would not be *him* who gave them away.

They stepped inside and were greeted with the sight of Harrison adjusting his hairpiece, which offset his gruff exterior and stern expression. Though an older man, he was still powerfully built, and his body matched his iron will.

The hairpiece only meant one thing, "News conference tonight, Commissioner?" Burke ventured.

"You got that right. I've gotta put out another statement on this Wraith character. Assure the public we're doing everything in our power to apprehend him, Metro City deserves better than vigilante justice, blah, blah, blah." Harrison trailed off as he finished with his hairpiece. "Which tie do you guys like better?" The Commissioner said as he held up two ties: one olive and the other crimson.

"Olive, definitely," Wilcox said with false confidence. The detective really did not care, he wanted out of that office as fast as possible. Burke was doing the better job of being inconspicuous, not him. Erring on the side of caution, Wilcox decided to speak only when spoken to.

"Is there anything you wanted to see us about or was it just for fashion advice?" Burke said with a smile.

"Yes, I have an assignment for you. We may have a lead on one of Latham's smuggling operations. I want you guys to question a warehouse owner at this address." Harrison handed Wilcox the paper while he adjusted the olive tie.

"Why us?" Burke asked. "Isn't this Sloan and Perez's area?" Wilcox looked over at Burke. His voice sounded normal, but his eyes betrayed his paranoia.

"I sent them on another assignment. Now you two had better book it, our informant is getting nervous."

Burke and Wilcox had left the office and drove to the warehouse. Looking back on everything, Wilcox felt that Harrison sending them on this warehouse errand was the nail in the coffin.

"Hey, Burke?" Wilcox started, "Something feels wrong to you about today? Or is it just me?"

"Yeah, I know what you mean. Something's felt strange the whole day. I just can't put my finger on it." Burke confirmed.

"You think it's the heat? I know the heat drives my brother crazy, makes him act all loony and weird. Maybe it's just the heat." Wilcox said, trying to convince both of them.

"Yeah, maybe..." Burke doubted.

"You don't think Harrison knows, do you?" Wilcox blurted out.

"Well, who can blame us for being on the take? People spit on us every time we walk the streets, nobody respects us, and we don't get paid enough for putting ourselves on the line every day! Latham's money has finally started to put me ahead. The way I look at it, it's a matter of survival. Who could fault us for that?" Burke ranted. Wilcox remembered the rant well. It had been the same one Burke used to convince Wilcox to join him as a dirty cop.

"But you haven't answered my question. Do you think Harrison knows about us?" Wilcox pressed again.

Burke paused before he spoke. "No. Think about it: if Harrison really suspected Latham was paying us off, do you think that he'd send us to investigate Latham's operations?"

"No... no, that's true." Wilcox said. For the first time that day, the detective felt himself relax.

"Talk about counterproductive!" Burke said as the two shared a laugh.

Yet neither could completely escape the feeling that they were headed for an inevitable collision with fate.

●●●

Burke and Wilcox parked near the warehouse and got out of their car, stretching their legs and examining the area. Harrison had sent them to a downtrodden part of Metro City, infamous for two things: it was a haven for seedy activity and there were rumors of The Wraith lurking in the district. Though the police officials relentlessly denied his existence, some members of the force decided to confront the fact that there was a rouge vigilante operating in their city... and frankly doing a better job than they were. Not taking the matter lightly, Metro City had issued an arrest warrant for The Wraith, but apprehending him seemed nigh-impossible. If one listened to all of the wild stories about The Wraith, he could be a demon with supernatural powers. As usual, Wilcox felt compelled to utter his paranoid thoughts to Burke.

"What if The Wraith is here?" Wilcox whispered, sounding as though he thought the dread avenger was standing behind him.

"So what? He doesn't go after cops, so we're safe. He'll think we're on the same side." Burke said, feigning courage once more.

"But what if he knows we're working with Latham?" Wilcox protested.

"He will if you keep bringing it up! Neither of us are going to talk, period. Now let's have a little chat with the informant and get this over with." Burke said as he opened the door and peered inside the decrepit structure.

The first thing they were greeted with was a couple of rats scurrying into the shadows. The vermin's presence was indicative of the state of their surroundings. Broken boxes, unsold merchandise, and a veritable maze of cobwebs coating every corner of the warehouse.

"Hello?" Burke called out, not really expecting to get an answer. He turned to Wilcox with a suspicious expression, "What the hell are we doing here? This place has been abandoned for god knows how long?"

"Harrison's setting us up! He knows!" Wilcox shouted as he ran to the door. "Let's get the hell out of here!"

Wilcox twisted the doorknob, but found to his horror that it was inexplicably locked! He stepped back from it, and turned to Burke, his face pale with terror. "Neither of us locked this... right?"

"Well that's... um..." Burke started, but could not invent an explanation that could put either of them at ease. Glancing around, Burke saw a boarded up window and waved Wilcox over. "Here, we just yank a few of these boards out and we can get out through the window!"

Wilcox and Burke pushed a few of the sturdier boxes over to the window, and Burke climbed on top of them. Wrapping his hands around the wood, he attempted to pull the boards loose, but was struggling.

"You wanna give me a hand? What are you doing just standing there!" Burke snapped.

"Yeah, sure... it's just been bothering me though, who locked the door?" Wilcox voiced aloud.

"*I did!*"

Both men stopped moving and quickly glanced about the warehouse, searching for the owner of the voice. It was a cold and menacing voice, one that implied great power. Through the shadows, Wilcox could have sworn that he saw a large, caped figure watching them!

"It's him! It's The Wraith! Harrison knows, Burke! He set us up!" Wilcox yelled as he yanked his pistol out of his holster and started firing at the caped figure.

"Stop it, you idiot! You're firing at thin air! Burke wrenched the gun away from Wilcox and slapped him, trying to get his partner to cool down. The two looked over where Wilcox had opened fire and saw plenty of fresh bullet holes, but no bloodstains or signs of The Wraith.

"But you... you heard his voice, right? He's here!" Wilcox said defensively.

"Yeah, so help me get these damn boards down and we can get out of here!" Burke commanded.

Wilcox looked back from the spot and focused on Burke, but he instantly regretted doing that. The detective saw the same large, caped figure draped in midnight blue and black, standing behind Burke. It was The Wraith! Swifter than Wilcox could speak, The Wraith grabbed Burke, hoisted him over his head, and hurled him into a pile of boxes. The impact rendered Burke unconscious.

Wilcox raised his pistol but realized he had wasted all of his bullets as his gun emitted nothing but cold clicking noises. With a firm, iron grip, The Wraith twisted Wilcox's wrist, forcing him to drop the weapon. Though The Wraith's face was hidden behind a cowl, Wilcox could see the fury and disdain in his eyes. A strange glow from The Wraith's chest emblem caught Wilcox's attention, and he dared glance at the energy force that was gathering strength.

"Are you going to kill me?" Wilcox said, his voice wavering.

"Worse," was The Wraith's reply.

Then Wilcox realized what he was in store for. He had heard rumors of criminals confessing to police because of what they saw in The Wraith's Judgment Stare. None were quite sure how it worked, but Wilcox was about to find out first hand.

"The people of Metro City rely on you to keep them safe!" The Wraith began his sermon, his voice growing in intensity. "You have betrayed the people's trust when you sold your soul to Latham! You've taken money to turn a blind eye to his crimes, and *this* is how it feels!"

Wilcox felt as if his legs were broken like he was dropped from a great height. He wanted to scream, but the pain was overwhelming. "You have felt the pain of a man who refused to pay Latham's protection fee! When he called the police, you 'lost' the report, leading to that man's suffering!"

The Wraith's Judgment Stare was not limited to merely physical torture, far from it. Wilcox then suddenly felt a powerful mixture of despair, desperation, and fear. "A family had their store burned down. It was their chance at a better life! When you were called upon to investigate, Latham's money made you label it as 'an accident', letting the criminal go free!"

Several more horrific incidents were inflicted upon Wilcox, each one worst than the last. The Wraith stood over Wilcox's beaten, battered, and mentally tortured body. "Think of all the pain and suffering that you could have prevented if you had done your job! You are unworthy of the badge you wear!" The Wraith yelled as he ripped the badge from Wilcox's jacket and cast it aside.

Burke had woken up by this time, and witnessed the end of the Judgment Stare. He slowly tried to crawl away, but The Wraith turned to face him. The vigilante strode over, his eyes narrowing with fury, his chest beginning to glow once again.

"Wait! Wait!" Burke protested. "I know something that could help you! You—you're after cops like us, right! Well—I can tell you a few things about us! We've got something *big* planned!"

The Wraith paused, his chest stopped glowing. "Tell me," The Wraith commanded.

The dread avenger listened with rapt attention as Burke launched into a plan that even surprised the vigilante. After Burke gave the details, he watched as The Wraith nodded grimly.

"So... I get something for coming clean, right? I mean, you wouldn't have known about this without me? So can you let me go? I swear I'll be an honest cop from now on!" Burke yammered and yelled, though at this point he would have said anything to escape from The Wraith.

To his dismay, The Wraith's chest began to glow once again. "Nobody escapes justice. Nobody."

●●●

Detective Rosa Perez wedged into her booth at Maxwell Diner, the red vinyl of the seat sticking to her uncomfortably. Despite her attractive features, she had a hard edge about her that intimidated many people. She looked across the table at her partner, Bob Sloan, who had a similar disposition. The two of them had many years on the force between them, and had seen every type of criminal from a street pusher to the evil leader of a long lost Aztec tribe.

Yet, both of them were undeniably tense. Sloan broke the ice by simply asking:

"Why here? Couldn't we have done this in her office?"

"Apparently not," Perez said as she pretended to be interested in an advertisement for the diner's summer special. They were meeting with someone named Layla Roscoe from internal affairs. Many officers and detectives in the Metro City Police Department were openly hostile to internal affairs. The corrupt ones were suspicious of them and the honest ones were resentful that they were under suspicion. The two of them fell into the latter category, and Sloan and Perez wondered what she had in store for them.

"If she's going to try and blackmail us, she's wasting her time." Sloan grunted after he took a sip of coffee.

"Blackmail us for what? Your use of excessive force? There's no secret in that." Perez rolled her eyes. "Honestly, Bob, you expect the worst from *everybody.*"

Sloan nodded with a shrug. Having learned Sloan's body language over the years, Perez knew exactly what that gesture meant. Sloan knew she was right, and that was his way of conceding defeat without having to admit that he was wrong.

At that moment, a nervous looking woman in a business suit hurried over to their table. "Um, excuse me. Detectives Robert Sloan and Rosa Perez?" she spoke quickly. The detectives looked up at Layla and quickly appraised her. Short, spiked hair, glasses and a bulge underneath her jacket. Both of them knew she was carrying a concealed weapon and was not used to it. Obviously, she felt she needed some kind of protection.

"I'm Perez," she said, shaking her hand, "you wanted to see us Ms. Roscoe?"

"Yes," she replied while looking out the windows hastily, trying to spot anything suspicious. Not seeing anything that made her suspicious, she sat down and drummed her fingers on the tabletop.

"Relax, you're making *me* nervous," Sloan said. He consciously took a bit of the edge off of his voice, attempting to calm Layla.

"If you're nervous now, I can't imagine what you're going to be feeling when I tell you this," Layla said as she pulled out a file from the briefcase she was carrying. "For the record, I told nobody I was coming here."

"You asked for us specifically, why?" Perez enquired as she took the file from Layla.

"While I was doing research, I decided I could trust you two, and you also have the most influence with Commissioner Harrison."

"Even with *my* record?" Sloan said, surprised that she did not hold his many ticks of police brutality and suspect complaints against him.

"You've always done, or at least tried to do the right thing, Detective Sloan. And you, Detective Perez, are an honest officer through-and-through. I know it's been tough, and the police department has an unwritten code of silence, but you have been unafraid to speak out against your fellow officers." This part of her speech appeared rehearsed, and it probably was, but it seemed to calm her.

"Is that what this is about?" Sloan asked. "You want us to look into one of our own guys? I thought that was *your* job."

"It is, but this is bigger than just one officer... or even a small group of them," Layla explained. Sloan glanced over at Perez, and saw her mouth gape as she looked through Layla's files. They were profile sheets and records of many Metro City police officers. It looked like most of the duty roster was on there.

"We know there is undeniable corruption within the department, but to imagine that it's gone this far..." Perez said in disgust. There were some officers that everybody *knew* were corrupt, some that were only suspected, but the worst were the ones that she assumed were friends. "And you can be sure of all this? Because if you are wrong..."

"I wish I was, but this represents a majority of the police force," Layla said.

"Latham... we'll get that piece of trash one day!" Sloan vowed through gritted teeth.

"I've been tracking the activities of some of the more, shall we say, prominent members of this group. They've been meeting more often than usual, and the number of people involved in these meetings is growing." Layla explained.

"I'll bet this isn't some after-hours social club," Sloan scoffed.

"Why have we never heard of these meetings? We're cops." Perez asked, confused. Then the answer came to her and she sighed, "Of course, we're honest cops."

"Look through the file. They're mobilizing, planning to make a move," Layla suggested, a sense of urgency emerging in her voice.

"There's something I do not understand. Why not go to Commissioner Harrison directly? Why talk to us first?" Perez said, handing the folder over to Sloan.

"If the conspirators knew that I knew... they'd kill me. Not to mention that Internal Affairs is not exactly a respected branch of the department.

I doubt he'd..."

Bright headlights suddenly cut across the diner, and the sharp sound of wheels screaming on the road silenced their conversation. Layla, Perez, and Sloan looked over to see a dark sedan speeding by the alley and a man leaning out of the passenger's seat. A metal glint betrayed the assault rifle in his hands, and Sloan reacted instantly.

"Get down!" he yelled as he leaped across the table. He knew Perez could take care of herself, but had his doubts about Layla. Sloan was desperate to shield Layla from the hail of bullets.

The machine gun opened fire, muzzle flashes lighting the area with a bright yellow glow. Patrons and staff screamed as the bullets shredded the glass windows. Debris was flying everywhere, joined by splintered fragments of exploding dishes and orange sparks bouncing off of the metal kitchen surfaces. Sloan had made it over the table, and wrapped his arms around Layla's head, protecting her from harm. However, a sharp scream emitted from Layla, and Sloan knew he was too late.

Perez, having hidden underneath the window sill, watched as Layla and Sloan toppled to the ground. She knew that she was unharmed, but worried about Layla and the other patrons. Perez heard the car speed away as she rushed over to check on Layla. Perez saw the Internal Affairs officer had taken a bullet to her shoulder, and Layla was beginning to tremble and stutter violently. She was going into shock. One glance at Sloan's face and Layla knew that despite his training, he was not suited to handle this.

"Get out of my way!" Perez snapped in a commanding tone, and Sloan obligingly jumped out of the way. "I'll take care of her! Get after them! Now!" She commanded.

Sloan nodded, getting up and looking around the diner. Mercifully, no one appeared to be dead or seriously injured, but with everyone slowly recovering, it would take Sloan too long to navigate through the sea of people. With no time to waste, Sloan jumped through the broken window and raced towards his car. He looked across the street, and saw that the dark sedan was still within eyesight, its red taillights swerving through the traffic ahead. Sloan threw open his car door, and fired up the engine as he placed the portable police light on the roof. He did not have much optimism with his chances of stopping traffic with the siren though, because the assassins had driven onto the freeway!

Racing through traffic, Sloan was gaining on the hitman's car. He was about to radio for assistance, but he remembered Layla's warning about his fellow officers. It disturbed him to think he was all alone, and he was potentially in pursuit of people whom he served with. When they opened fire, they were aiming for Layla, but were unconcerned with the lives of the people in the diner.

That infuriated him, and he pushed the gas pedal down even further. The hitmen's car, in an effort to lose Sloan, desperately swerved into the oncoming traffic lane. Despite the late hour, traffic was flowing rapidly, and each car was a new, deadly projectile hurled at Sloan. Sloan swerved back and forth, his knuckles turning white as his hands tightened around the steering wheel. Whoever was driving the hitmen's car was a professional, and it took everything Sloan had to keep on his tail.

An unexpected cracking noise made Sloan's heart leap! He allowed himself a fleeting glance and discovered that he had passed too close to a large truck, which violently knocked the passenger side mirror from his car! The dark sedan seemed to navigate through the high-speed maze with expert precision. Sloan knew that he had been lucky so far, but how long could that hold out?

It dawned on Sloan that following the would-be assassins was not the answer. He needed to pull past them, but saw that construction ahead prevented him from going into a safer lane. There was a brief lull in the traffic that allowed him to think clearly: the road they were racing along only had one exit! All Sloan had to do was find a quick path and block the exit. Stopping them would not be easy, from what he could tell, there were at least three men in the car, and one of them had a loaded machine gun.

As if echoing his thoughts, he could discern that the hitmen were shifting around in the car ahead of him. Instinctively, he took one hand off the steering wheel and grabbed his pistol, waiting for them to make their move. A moment later, a masked man stuck his head out of the car and aimed the machine gun at Sloan! The detective ducked down as he swerved, managing to avoid the volley of gunfire. He heard metal clanking and glass cracking as bullets nailed his car. Though crouched, Sloan had allowed himself enough room to see over the dashboard. Through this narrow opening, Sloan discerned that the assassin was reloading, and Sloan seized the opportunity!

Gunning his car forward, Sloan was soon parallel with the dark sedan! Raising his pistol, he proceeded to empty the clip into the hitman's car, hoping to either hit one of them, or pop the tires. Sloan made the driver panic and start to weave around, but was unsure if he did any damage.

However, by being parallel, Sloan was forced to divide his attention between the road and the hitmen. It was not long before he realized that it was impossible to do both. He looked to make sure the road was relatively clear, but when he looked back to the dark sedan, Sloan realized

SLOAN WAS GAINING ON THE HITMAN'S CAR.

his mistake! The assassin's car had deliberately swerved towards him. The detective braced himself but it was too late. The cars collided, and Sloan lost control of his vehicle!

He struggled to gain control while bracing himself for the inevitable impact.

It came, and it was more tremendous than Sloan could have imagined. The hitmen had forced his car against the concrete barrier of the freeway. He felt every bone shake and his teeth rattle when he collided. The world seemed like it was on a dark, twisted, merry-go-round as Sloan fought for control.

When Sloan eventually stopped, he was aware of three things: the smoke from under his car hood meant that his engine was gone, he had the worst headache of his life, and the dark sedan had pulled up near him. The cars around them had also stopped, but people were abandoning their vehicles and fleeing the scene, screaming. It was not hard to see why. The three masked hitmen, all with machine guns, were running towards him.

"Who the hell is that anyway?" Sloan heard one of the assassins ask.

"Sloan." Another hitman said.

"Always hated that guy." The first voice replied. He heard clicking and the sounds of guns cocking.

In Metro City, a cop's life is a short one. Sloan was amazed that he had lasted this long. This was not the fate that he had envisioned for himself, and he worried about Perez. They would come for her next, and he would die knowing that he had failed her.

Moments before the end, fate took another detour. Small explosions erupted around the three hitmen, but they were not gunshots. Instead, a giant cloud of grey smoke filled the air, much to the annoyance and distraction of the would-be killers.

"What's going on?" one of them yelled.

"Who did that?" another demanded, fear creeping into his voice.

The third hitman never got a chance to speak. Instead, his cohorts heard the sound of a scream! Through the smoke, they could faintly discern a large, dark, caped figure fighting with their cohort. His yell was due to the fact that the mysterious figure had just broken his knee. He was silenced by a quick neck chop from The Wraith. His chest glowed ominously through the smoke, acting as a sinister warning light to the criminals.

"Who the hell are you?" the terrified henchman yelled.

"It's The Wraith, you idiot! Kill him!" his compatriot squealed in fear.

The task was easier said than done, for The Wraith pounced upon them with the grace and power of a jungle cat. Quickly disarming both of them, The Wraith immediately went for crippling blows. He broke the first assassin's arms and proceeded to knock the wind out of him with a swift kick to the chest. With that, he turned his attention to the last hitman. The poor fellow, now consumed with fear, dropped to his knees and begged for mercy.

"Please, Mr. Wraith! They would have killed me if I didn't cooperate! Please! I have a family, don't kill me!"

The Wraith advanced on him, his jaw set grimly. His chest began to glow with power as he glared at the sniveling, pathetic figure before him.

"Do you think pleading will help you? You are wrong."

Thus, another criminal was a victim of the Judgment Stare. While the hitman was being tortured, Sloan was able to slowly climb out of his now mangled car. The detective took a quick appraisal of himself underneath the orange glow of a streetlight. His clothing was torn up and disheveled. Sloan had plenty of bruises that were beginning to smart, and several cuts that needed medical attention, but he would have to fight through it. People needed him.

Sloan looked up and saw the third hitman drop, the Judgment Stare having ended. The vigilante and the detective faced each other once again. Their relationship had always been tense at best and a game of cat-and-mouse at worst. In the beginning, Sloan had voiced disdain for vigilantism. The very idea that a self-appointed avenger was undermining what he and the honorable police officers fought to create was despicable to the detective. When The Wraith had moved from being an urban legend to an open case, Sloan was eager to lead the charge to apprehend the dread avenger. Sloan felt betrayed when he found out that Commissioner Harrison had privately been a supporter of The Wraith.

Eventually, Detective Sloan was forced to eat crow and acknowledge that, despite his reservations, The Wraith was a force of good in Metro City. He was determined to find out who was behind the mask, but that would have to wait. There were far more pressing matters at hand.

"Wraith..." Sloan began awkwardly as their eyes met. The dread avenger's gaze was unnerving, even without any of his mystical powers. "Thank you for that, I owe you my life."

"Are you hurt?" The Wraith asked, more for utilitarian purposes than actual concern.

"I'll live. Listen, Wraith, something big is going down." Sloan started, realizing that the vigilante's appearance was perfectly timed.

"I know. There is going to be a coup in the Metro City Police Headquarters.

The worst among you are getting ready to overthrow Commissioner Harrison." The Wraith said firmly.

"Oh my god... What can we do?" Sloan gasped.

"I'll need your help navigating through the police headquarters. Can I count on you?" The Wraith pressed.

"It's not like we have a choice," Sloan said.

•••

"She's stabilized for now!" one medic shouted to another over the roar of the ambulance. "But she's gotta go into ER right away!"

Two EMT workers labored feverishly to keep Layla alive. A flash of her detective's badge earned Perez a ride in the ambulance. Based on what Layla had told them, she placed a call to Commissioner Harrison. Perez waited anxiously on the end of the phone; each dial tone making her heart beat faster. Why was he not picking up?

"He could be away from his phone..." Perez tried to tell herself "...*or he could be dead!*" It was a dark, fearful thought that despite her best efforts, she could not shake loose.

The detective looked down at Layla, her face was covered with an oxygen mask and her shoulder was plastered with an assortment of bandages. If these butchers were willing to sacrifice innocent lives to get their target, god knows what they were going to do to police headquarters!

"Commissioner Harrison," he answered his phone in his usual blunt manner.

"Thank god, Commissioner! It's Detective Perez and there's..." she began to speak. Perez was relieved to hear him, yet began to worry anew for his safety.

"Speak up! I can barely hear you!" Harrison barked. "Where are you?"

"I'm in an ambulance! A member of Internal Affairs was shot and I'm escorting her! You need to listen to me right now!"

"What's going on? Who are you talking about?" he demanded.

"No time to explain! They're after you! Get out of the building now!" Perez yelled.

Harrison was about to reply, but then his intercom sounded. He quickly answered it.

"What is it?"

"Commissioner, I'm the desk clerk from the armory. There is a large group of people appropriating SWAT gear and suits, saying that you authorized them, but I don't have anything on record. Did you..."

"How many people are there?" Harrison said, beginning to feel a cold chill running down his spine.

"I would guess thirty, but I don't see any training or operations scheduled... wait... what are you doing?" the desk clerk began to ask one of the officers he was speaking to. "What do you think you're...."

Gunfire and his screams emitted from Commissioner Harrison's speaker.

The coup was on.

"Get out of there, now!" Perez commanded, having heard the killing over the phone.

"And abandoned my men? Hell no! I'm in charge here, and I'm not going down without a fight! You keep that officer safe! Where is Sloan?"

"He was in pursuit of the trigger men. I have no idea where he is now." Perez admitted.

Harrison saw movement from the corner of his eye, and he looked up to see the tall silhouette of a man through the frosted glass window. The figure moved quickly and deliberately, and the Commissioner's instincts told him to prepare himself.

"I'll call you back," Harrison said as he quickly hung up with one hand, and grabbed his sidearm with the other. The door creaked open, and Harrison saw the lean, well-muscled figure of Gabe Rhodes enter the room. He had a five o'clock shadow, military-precise crew cut, and the darkness under his eyes indicated that the man had not rested in days. Harrison observed that Gabe was in his patrol uniform and that his gun was out!

Thinking quickly, Harrison snapped his arm up, leveling his weapon at Gabe. The would-be assassin looked surprised and instinctively put his hands up.

"Don't move!" Harrison commanded.

"Easy, easy there Commissioner," Gabe tried to reassure Harrison in his raspy voice, but the Commissioner did not budge.

"Close the door. Now!" Harrison barked, and Gabe obeyed. The door closed, but it did not block the sounds of screaming, yelling and occasional bursts of gunfire. It pained Harrison to hear that, but he forced himself to focus on Gabe.

"Gun on the table. I won't ask twice." Harrison said, intentionally keeping his voice calm and controlled, but with an edge of menace.

Again, Gabe followed the Commissioner's command and surrendered his weapon. "I don't know what you think you can accomplish here,

George. We have the building." Gabe spoke plainly, trying to undermine Harrison's confidence.

"I am the Commissioner. We're not equals, officer Rhodes." Harrison reminded him.

"We're in charge now. I'm in command, George." Gabe spoke cockily.

"Not from where I'm standing," Harrison said, checking the sights of his pistol. They were perfectly aligned with Gabe's chest as he stood defiantly.

"So, let's analyze this situation. You shoot me, then a bunch of my boys flood in here and mow you down. My second-in-command takes over, and I get what I want in the end... except the satisfaction of killing you myself." Gabe gave a small, condescending chuckle. "What's this standoff all about? Pride? Vanity? It's pointless, and frankly, embarrassing."

"What's embarrassing is seeing you in that uniform. You're not fit to be a cop." Harrison said.

"Not fit to be a..." Gabe trailed off before letting his disgust show through, "George, I don't know what freaking world you're living in, but as cops we don't make a dent in this city. The city turned on us a long time ago, and now we're taking it back!"

"How? By killing your own people?" Harrison shot back.

"It's called evolution, George! Survival of the fittest! There is a new vision for law and order in this city and they aren't a part of it. It's regrettable, but it had to be done!" Gabe exclaimed.

"Who's vision for the city? Latham's? Where the police run the extortion racket?" Harrison uttered with contempt.

Gabe smiled slyly at Commissioner Harrison. "We took out the recording devices in the building before this all started, so don't think you'll trick me into confessing anything." Gabe slowly sat down in the wooden chair opposite Harrison's desk and made an exaggerated act of settling in and relaxing. "If you were going to pull the trigger, you would have done it by now."

Harrison's finger hovered over the trigger while he contemplated his options. To his chagrin, Gabe was correct in his assessment. No matter what scenario he played out in his head, there was no way that Harrison could come out on top. Harrison's mind raced, there had to be a way...

●●●

Sloan found himself nervously loitering in a parking lot within sight of the Metro City Police Headquarters. He was a man of action, and being told to wait did not sit well with him. Nevertheless, The Wraith, thought Sloan was loathe to admit it, was the best chance they had for saving his fellow officers.

"Anything unusual?" The Wraith asked. The dread avenger had given Sloan an earpiece so he could alert him to any outside activity.

"Well, except for the armored men on patrol, I can't see anything unusual," Sloan reported.

"Keep your eyes open, I am heading in." The Wraith ordered.

"Wait, don't you think..." Sloan feebly began, but he saw that he was too late.

Sloan glimpsed the metallic sheen of a grappling hook as it was shot from the rooftop of a nearby building onto the roof of Police Headquarters. The line was pulled taut, and The Wraith slid along it seconds later. His cape flowing majestically against the sky, The Wraith moved with expert precision and coordination.

The dread avenger collected his grappling hook and rope, making his way towards the rooftop doorway. Sloan had provided The Wraith with a crudely drawn map of the building, and he activated his cowl's night vision to study it.

The Wraith reasoned his best course of action was to hide in the shadows and pounce on his targets. He would have to be swift and decisive, for any error or miscalculation would result in a dead police officer. The Wraith saw three SWAT officers patrolling the helipad, and quietly spoke to Sloan.

"Three men in heavy armor on the roof. Is that normal?"

"What? No, especially not in this weather. It's probably part of the coup, protecting all entrances and exits." Sloan said, craning his head and moving around in an attempt to get a better look.

The Wraith did not reply as he advanced towards the SWAT guard nearest him. He spied the second guard, who was loitering near the door. He was obviously relying on the other two to keep watch. The third sentry was a problem. Based on his posture and movements he was vigilant and eager for action.

Rolling out from behind his cover, The Wraith executed a perfect sweeping kick that knocked the first SWAT guard off his feet. Before he had a chance to call out, The Wraith was upon the downed sentry, his cape cloaking the two in shadow. A strong, well-practiced punch knocked his target unconscious, and The Wraith swiftly moved to take down the other guards.

He needed something that would clatter and draw attention, so he grabbed a metal ammunition clip from the first guard's vest pouch and threw it carefully. As The Wraith predicted, the clip made a great bedlam on the concrete helipad. The second sentry got his weapon ready, walking out to investigate the noise. The third guard, as the dread avenger suspected, was rooted firmly in place. Like a predatory animal, he was investigating the places that the second SWAT sentry was not. All The Wraith had to do was wait for his two enemies to align.

Once they did, The Wraith hurled his grappling hook at the third SWAT guard, and it clashed against the guard's helmet, forcing him off balance. The second guard wheeled around and aimed his weapon at The Wraith, giving him only seconds to act! The Wraith had pulled back on the grappling hook rope, causing the implement to race back towards him. The second guard was in the hook's path, and it swept him off his feet as it caught his legs!

The Wraith raced forward and stepped purposely onto the second sentry's body, causing him a great deal of pain. The dread avenger used the unfortunate sentry as a spring board to catapult himself at the third guard. The third SWAT officer had recovered from his dazed state, and was reaching for his gun. The Wraith knocked the weapon out of his hands with his fist, and threw a crippling strike at the one minimally armored place on the guard's body: the neck. Instantly, the third sentry stopped struggling, gasping for air. Yanking off the guard's helmet, the dread avenger pulled him into a rising knee strike to the head, knocking him unconscious.

The second guard was now getting up, having had the wind knocked out of him. As he stood, he was greeted by the frightening sight of The Wraith quickly bearing down on him. Before he could react, he felt his collar strain and tighten as the dread avenger hoisted him up off the ground, his feet no longer touching the ground

"Where are the other officers? The *honest* ones!" The Wraith growled in the petrified guard's face.

"We're... we took 'em to the evidence locker for uh... uh... 'indoctrination'!" The sentry offered before squealing, "Please don't kill me!"

"How many of you are there?" The Wraith demanded.

"Uh... thirty? I guess... I don't know! I'm cooperating here! Are you going to let me…"

The Wraith had what he needed, so an elbow to the sentry's face terminated the conversation. After using the guard's own handcuffs on them, The Wraith glanced at Sloan's map. He was displeased to learn that the Evidence Locker Room was underground, which was not ideal for a man standing on a rooftop. Still, The Wraith would have to make do and figure his way through.

He took a radio from one of the downed guards so he could eavesdrop on enemy communications. What he heard was also not to his liking, "So where's Gabe? We're waiting for him to give the order!" one of the corrupt cops whined.

"He's in Harrison's office! The commissioner and he are in some kinda standoff!" explained another.

"Are you kidding me? Any chance you could take him out, Nico?" yet another said.

"I'm circling around the side. Give me a minute and I'll have a clear shot!" was Nico's reply.

The Wraith glanced back at the map, estimated the most likely position for the shooter, and leapt into action!

Racing towards the edge of the roof, The Wraith peered over and saw that there was no awning or balcony for him to land on. The building, with the exception of the window sills, was a flat surface. There was no time for the stairs; Commissioner Harrison would be dead by then! The Wraith glanced at the map again and noticed that Harrison's office was a couple of floors down from the helipad. He knew what he had to do.

●●●

Perez was pacing back and forth in the Metro City Medical Center, her shoes making a hard clack on the floor as she circled the lobby. Layla was undergoing an operation in the emergency room, and though the doctors told Perez that she had a strong chance of pulling through, the detective was uncertain. Desperate to get a hold of any information, Perez called the one person that she knew she could trust: Sloan.

After a few tense rings, he picked up.

"Hello?" he sounded tired and on edge.

"It's Perez. What's going on?" she asked breathlessly.

"I'll tell you in a minute. How is Layla?" Sloan enquired.

"The doctors think that she'll live. They're removing the bullet and are going to put her under armed guard."

"Do we know anything about the guards?" Sloan exclaimed, a fear rushing through him. "We can't afford to have anything happen to her! If everything goes wrong here, she may be the only one who can keep this city together!"

"Yes, I checked them out and we can trust them. What's going on over there?" Perez said, a sinking feeling in her stomach.

"Well, headquarters is under siege by a group of corrupt cops who cleaned out the armory. They're all wearing SWAT gear. I'm stuck out here with no way to get in, and The Wraith's on the rooftop!" Sloan quickly summarized.

"The Wraith? What's he doing there?"

"I don't know how he found out about this, but he's interfering again." Sloan said, his feelings of disdain coming to the surface.

"At this point, we should take all the help we can get. Listen, do you think all the corrupt cops are in the building?" Perez asked, an idea dawning on her.

"I guess so. Probably all the ones involved in this coup are, I don't know about the small-time ones. What do you have in mind?" Sloan asked warily.

"I can get a call out to all the officers on patrol, the ones that we know we can trust, and get them to return to headquarters," Perez explained. "They can set up a barricade around the building."

"Cops fighting cops... what's the world coming to?" Sloan grumbled, but then a thought struck him "Hey, wait a minute! If we do that, then Metro City won't have a police patrol tonight! Do you realize what will happen?"

"Yes, and do you realize what will happen if the police fall under Latham's control?" Perez countered. "I know it's a tough call, but I think it's the best one."

"I understand that, but... what *is* he doing?" Sloan asked, exasperated.

"What's going on?" Perez said, alarmed.

"The Wraith! He's rappelling down the building!" Sloan exclaimed.

Indeed, The Wraith was using his grappling hook to descend a side of the building. His cape floated in the wind as he bounded downward with his powerful leg muscles. When he reached the area where he calculated the sniper might be, The Wraith paused only momentarily to get his bearings. The dread avenger's eyes narrowed as he spotted his target. One of the corrupted SWAT snipers, Nico, was readying his shot. The red laser point of his sniper rifle was aiming at Commissioner Harrison's figure through the frosted glass office window. He was getting ready to squeeze the trigger!

"Nico..." The Wraith spoke into his commandeered radio.

It was the delay that The Wraith needed. Nico took his hand from the trigger and put it to his headset. The vigilante did not pay attention to the sniper's response as he swung backwards, preparing to plunge through

"THE WRAITH! HE'S RAPPELLING DOWN THE BUILDING!"

the window and strike the assassin.

Nico was blindsided by The Wraith's assault! Shards of shattered glass flew in every direction as The Wraith's boots collided with the sniper's back. The blow knocked him off of his feet and threw him to the floor.

Inside Commissioner Harrison's office, the tides of war shifted yet again. The great crash from The Wraith's attack caused both Harrison and Gabe to look over. However, Gabe quickly took advantage of the situation and lunged at the Commissioner, his hands closing around Harrison's wrists. The two wrestled for control of Harrison's pistol, both men attempting to overpower each other. Gabe found himself surprised by the older man's strength, but he was holding his own. The gun fired several times, the thunder of each gunshot roaring in the small office while holes were violently punched into the ceiling. Commissioner Harrison and Gabe had rotated and changed positions several times during the struggle, and Harrison now found his back to the door.

Outside the office, The Wraith had heard the shots and was ready to rush over and provide assistance, but he stopped when he saw a group of SWAT officers rushing towards the noise. Even with his strength and gadgetry, the dread avenger knew that it was too risky to engage them while the lives of hostages were in the balance. The Wraith remembered that Commissioner Harrison was a capable man, and trusted he could take care of himself. Still, the vigilante decided to give him a fighting chance.

The Wraith checked his utility belt and saw, to his dismay, that he had only a small handful of smoke bombs left. They would have to do, and The Wraith would be forced to improvise his numerous getaways for the night. The dread avenger threw the bombs on the ground, where they exploded into a large, cumulous gray cloud. He heard the SWAT team complain that they could not see, and they began using their gun-mounted flashlights to cut through the artificial haze.

Commissioner Harrison realized that he was losing the battle, and decided, to his chagrin, that it would be best to flee. Harrison determined he could be more effective elsewhere. Seeing that the smoke was beginning to waft into his office, Harrison quickly jabbed his fist into Gabe's eye. The blow caused him to release his hold on Harrison, but Gabe managed to retain control of the gun. Harrison speedily flew out the door, dodging gunfire from Gabe as he yelled after him.

A deep, angry grunt came from the stairwell. Harrison could not be sure, but when he looked over, he thought that he saw a cape trailing off down the stairs. The Commissioner, reasoning that none of the traitorous officers would wear a cape, decided to follow the figure. He picked up an assault rifle from a fallen SWAT team member. Harrison surmised that it must have been The Wraith's handiwork, and raced down the stairs.

Gabe got on his radio and hollered to his men, "Track down the Commissioner! Now! Somebody patch me through on the intercom!"

A half-second later, another officer's voice came through on the radio, "You're on, sir."

"George, listen up! We've captured the police force in the building. If you don't surrender yourself, we're going to kill one of them every ten minutes!" Gabe barked before turning off his radio.

He caught the stare of one of his men, looking surprised at Gabe's declaration. Gabe sneered at him, "Survival of the fittest. You got a problem with that?"

●●●

"I assume you heard that," The Wraith said over the radio. Sloan was itching for action, growing angry for remaining on the sidelines. The detective had seen The Wraith go through the window, heard the roar of gunfire, watched the smoke rise from the shattered window, and felt his heart freeze upon hearing Gabe's ultimatum. Sloan could not have felt more useless.

"Yes! Yes of course I heard it! Now what can I..." The detective yelled at The Wraith, but he found himself distracted. "Hang on!"

Sloan watched as a convoy of police cars blazed towards him, their sirens were wailing through the night while their lights slashed red and blue streaks down the streets of Metro City. The cars pulled around the station and formed a barricade around police headquarters. Perez got out of the lead car and briskly walked over to Sloan.

"That's everyone, Bob. We have enough people to cover the building, but that's it." Perez briefed him.

Sloan was about to respond, but The Wraith chimed in, "What was that?"

"We have the building surrounded, Wraith. Detective Perez called every honest cop on patrol and had them come back." Sloan explained.

"I see. I need your help, Detective Sloan," The Wraith began.

"Yeah, well about time I was of some use..." Sloan began, but then he noticed that The Wraith sounded different. His voice was husky and his breathing labored. "Is everything alright?"

"I'm fine. I'm heading towards the hostages, but I need you to do something about the lights. Knock out the generator." The Wraith commanded.

"Knock out the..." Sloan began incredulously, "How on earth do you expect me to do that? You think I'm an electrician? Not to mention that everyone in the building would be gunning for me!"

"You will find a way." The Wraith then deactivated his radio, and Sloan turned to Perez.

"What's going on here? What's The Wraith doing?" Perez asked, her mind swimming with questions.

"I'll explain on the way, but we need to get to the generator room and kill the power. The Wraith needs us to knock out the lights." Sloan shouted.

"The Wraith, you trust him now?" Perez said dubiously.

"He's helping the hostages, and he's our best shot right now. Like you said, we should take any break we can get." Sloan shrugged, and then he checked his watch, "We have to hurry, we've only got... eight minutes before Gabe executes one of the hostages!"

●●●

The Wraith had found refuge inside of a cramped, metal ventilation shaft. His mind was locked with inner turmoil as he made his way through the duct system. Though his suit had absorbed most of the damage, The Wraith had been shot while trying to make his escape. He was now in an unoccupied area of Police Headquarters. The Wraith would have the opportunity to remove the bullet from his side, thus enabling him to fight more effectively.

However, he would be sacrificing time necessary to save the hostages. Even if he managed to patch himself up, The Wraith risked not being there for the people that desperately needed him! If he managed to arrive in time, how useful could he be with a serious injury? The dread avenger wrestled with these questions for a moment, before deciding that he must forgo removing the bullet. Saving innocent people always came first.

As he crawled silently through the ducts, the vigilante's mind drifted to thoughts of death. The Wraith was well acquainted with mortality. It was through the demise of The Wraith that came before him that granted him his mystical, mysterious powers. It was seemingly that way with each passing Wraith. One passed on before another could take his place. The Wraith was wondering, if anything happened to him, who would be the one to take his place? Sloan, Perez, maybe...

No! The Wraith would not permit himself to venture beyond that speculation! Any further and he would be admitting the possibility of defeat. It was not an option when lives were in the balance.

Using his night vision, The Wraith unfolded Sloan's map and looked upon it once more. He was further away from the evidence storage than he liked, and he estimated that he had about five minutes left. Unfortunately, the sound of heavy footsteps and clinking armor forced The Wraith to stop moving, for the vigilante realized that two men were walking underneath him. He looked through the thin lines of ventilation, and beheld two SWAT officers patrolling the halls. They were hunched over, their weapons pointed forward and the two seemed ready for action.

"I swear I saw him run through here!" one of them griped.

"You sure Harrison can still run? Thought he was a desk jockey," the other officer quipped.

"Yeah, well, I guess that old man can still fight. Beat the crap out of Gabe!" the first officer chuckled.

"So what do we do when we find him? Bring him back or...?"

"I say we shoot him. Hey, I don't owe Harrison any favors. Between you and me I've got friends down there, and we've got five minutes before one of them dies if Harrison is still around!" the first officer exclaimed, to the surprise of the second officer.

"I thought you agreed to this! Are you trying to back out?"

"Yeah, I did... but... I keep thinking that if one of them dies it's my fault! They are my friends." the first officer explained, though it did not seem to appease the second officer.

"Gabe made this clear! If you are not with us, you're against us! Now..."

"Wraith! Wraith are you there?" Sloan's voice crackled over The Wraith's radio. Though it was normally undetectable, being trapped in a small, metal corridor amplified the sound and caught the attention of the two SWAT men underneath the dread avenger! They looked up at the ventilation shaft, their eyes wide with surprise.

"What is going on?" snapped the second officer.

His cover was blown! The Wraith had to act swiftly, so he hit the grate with a powerful punch! The blow wrenched apart that section of the ventilation, and the dread avenger leapt out and landed on the second SWAT officer. The Wraith did not have time for anything fancy; he simply clocked the man as hard as he could with his rock hard fist. The officer was out instantly, to the relief of The Wraith, for he could feel intense pain in his side as a result of the motion. The vigilante knew that he could not rely on his martial arts prowess, and that he would need to use intimidation and ingenuity to save the hostages.

The Wraith rounded on the first SWAT officer, and based on the conversation he had overheard, judged him to be the more compassionate of the two. Deciding that he would force him to cooperate, The Wraith shot out his arm and seized his target by the throat, pinning him to the wall.

"What's your name?" The Wraith demanded.

"T...Tyler..." was the weak, frightened reply.

"The captives! How many are guarding them?" The Wraith growled through tightly gritted teeth. He regretted not having time to inflict the Judgment Stare on Tyler.

"Three... three in the room. I can help you if you let me go!" Tyler blurted.

The Wraith knew that this was a plea born of desperation, and doubted if Tyler could be an asset. Deciding not to take the risk, The Wraith headbutted the corrupt officer. He fell to the floor, blood slowly oozing from his nose.

Remembering that it was Sloan's call that had revealed his presence, The Wraith activated his radio once more. "I'm here, detective. Talk."

"Perez and I managed to sneak into the building; we are heading for the power generator now. One of the cops outside said the backup generator will kick in one minute after it is knocked out, so that's all the time we can buy you." Sloan explained, trying to keep his voice down.

"That's fine. Commissioner Harrison is still in the building. Keep him safe if you find him." The Wraith ordered and he silenced his radio for the time being. In the dread avenger's estimation, the ventilation ducts were still the safest means of transportation, so The Wraith decided to keep traveling through them.

●●●

In the depths of the Metro City Police Headquarters, Sloan and Perez stealthily moved along a deserted corridor. Sloan had viewed these halls, and this building, as a safe haven from the world outside. It was an eerie, alien feeling to him to see this environment as hostile, where every shadow could conceal a threat. He glanced at a wall clock and felt a new wave of anxiety wash over him.

"We only have six minutes!" Sloan whispered to Perez.

She nodded, "Do you have any idea how to turn a power generator off?"

"We're going to have to figure it out when we get there. I hope there's some kind of master switch or control panel." Sloan replied.

As they raced down the hallway, Perez pointed excitedly to some stenciled words on the wall.

"There! There's the generator room! We still have time to..." she began, but trailed off as a shadowy figure came around the corner.

It went against instinct, but Sloan and Perez forced themselves to raise their weapons at the approaching SWAT officer. They were quicker on the draw, and the officer was stunned.

"Rosa... Bob?" the officer asked in amazement. Perez recognized the voice and was visibly shaken.

"Jane? Oh god, not you!" the detective shuddered in disbelief.

Jane had her hands up, and slowly, carefully removed her helmet. They saw her round face, with her dark, gentle eyes. It had once been a friendly face, one of the few that both Sloan and Perez thought they could trust. Sloan was disgusted by this attempted manipulation. Jane was outmanned and outgunned, so her last line of defense was to pull at their heartstrings? He would have none of it.

"Get out of our way!" Sloan snarled.

"I can't let you pass," Jane said uneasily. Clearly this was difficult for her as well.

"Do you know what's going on upstairs! Gabe is going to kill one of us! We're trying to fix this, help us!" Perez pleaded.

"You want to make things right? Find Harrison and bring him to Gabe, *that* will save the hostages!" Jane said, a streak of defiance in her voice.

"We don't have time to talk! Don't make me shoot!" Sloan threatened. Though the SWAT armor was solid and protective, Sloan spotted a weak spot in the ankle. It would be enough to bring her down without killing her. Perez looked over to Sloan, unsure of what to do.

"You shoot me, and then everyone in the generator room will come out, guns blazing!" Jane calmly, but firmly explained.

"You're bluffing!" Sloan spat.

"Try me, Bob!" Jane snapped back.

"Why are you doing this? We were your friends!" Perez implored.

"I'm doing this for you! For every cop! We can't beat Latham! God knows how long the entire force has been trying! Then some damned mystery man appears and shows Metro City how pathetic we are! Don't you realize that if we team up with Latham, so many problems will be solved? There will be no more gang wars between us and his men..." Jane started to repeat the same pitch that she was probably given.

"Right, because the cops *are* the gang," Sloan scoffed.

Jane glared at him, "Not to mention the fact that we'd actually be getting paid what we're worth!"

"And you'd sacrifice the life of someone you work with for a larger paycheck? I just want to make that clear." Sloan said, seeing how far he could push Jane.

"Gabe told us that it wouldn't be easy... and that there would be sleepless nights, but in the end, the ends do justify the means." Jane was not going for Sloan's bait.

"I hope so. Sorry, Jane." Perez said before she pulled the trigger!

Jane's boot ripped open, and she crumpled to the floor. Before she could emit an agonizing shriek, Perez raced over and kicked Jane in the face. Sloan grimaced at the gruesome sound, and quickly moved by Perez as she handcuffed Jane. The detective turned his head around the corner, but could not see anyone in the generator room.

"Jane *was* bluffing," Sloan sighed. "I knew it."

"She slowed us up! We only have four minutes to figure out how this machine works!" Perez reminded her partner as the two raced to the generator room.

●●●

Silent as a ghost's shadow, The Wraith crawled towards the end of the ventilation shaft and looked into the evidence room. The pain in his side was throbbing worse than before, but the dread avenger forced himself to ignore it. He was greeted by the sight of twenty or so police officers clustered together in the center of the room. Tyler was true to his word, for he saw three SWAT officers patrolling the perimeter with automatic weapons trained on the group. The Wraith observed that if any of the captives had tried to rush their captors, then the entire group would have certainly been killed.

The many shelves of evidence, all tagged and filed away, had been forcibly pushed to the perimeter of the room. This prevented any captives from trying to grab something that could have been useful, but it also gave The Wraith an advantage. One of the patrolling guards was standing close enough that The Wraith, once he removed the grating, could topple a shelf onto him. But what about the other two? He knew that he did not have much time left, so he quietly, carefully began to remove the grate. The dread avenger hoped that Sloan and Perez would come through any second, because after he took the first sentry, he doubted if he could rely on hand-to-hand combat skills with his wound.

One of the guard's radios crackled to life and she answered, "Yes, sir?"

"This is team leader. Grab one of the hostages and put him on the radio." The Wraith recognized the voice as belonging to Gabe, and knew that the poor prisoner's execution was only moments away! He could delay no longer, and then thought of a way to deal with the guards!

Remembering that he had lifted a radio from a sentry on the rooftop, The Wraith activated it and placed it near the narrow, metal walls of the ventilation ducts. Then the dread avenger removed his grappling hook and scraped it along the metal surface, right next to the microphone.

The dreadful, shrieking cacophony that the hook made against the metal caused the three guards to clutch at their ears, a temporary distraction that The Wraith needed. The vigilante burst forth from his hiding place and knocked one of the shelves onto the captor closest to him. He was down, but the remaining captors wheeled around, their weapons trained on him!

It was to his great fortune that the lights suddenly went out, leaving the room in total darkness. "Rush them!" The Wraith bellowed, and he could hear the sounds of a great scuffle as he climbed back up to the ventilation duct. Through his night vision, The Wraith could see that the captives had risen up to subdue their jailers and were now in possession of their weapons.

"What do we do now?" one of the police officers asked.

"There are too many of them for us to take on, so we'd better get out of here." another police officer answered.

"A while ago I heard a bunch of sirens approaching, maybe they're still out there!" yet another officer said optimistically.

The Wraith listened as the group decided to make a break for it and rendezvous with the other police officers at the barricade, where they would arm themselves and storm headquarters, taking it back by force. This sounded reasonable to The Wraith, but he was still wary of Commissioner Harrison's safety, and the fact that Gabe might have another trick up his sleeve.

It was time to cut the head off the serpent and deal with Gabe. The dread avenger instinctually knew that it was Latham, and not Gabe, who was the mastermind behind this plan. Therefore, Latham would have had

"WHAT DO WE DO NOW?"

some means of escape should anything go awry. With a barricade around the police headquarters, the only logical option was the roof, and his bet was that there would be a helicopter waiting to save Gabe.

The Wraith would not let that happen.

•••

Perez and Sloan raced from the generator room, having completed their task. Both of them were silent, hoping against hope that they switched off the lights in time. The entire police headquarters had temporarily been plunged into darkness, but the emergency generator came to life a minute later. It was an auxiliary supply, so the lights were only at minimum power. Deep, shadowy pools existed between these small beacons, resembling a highway at midnight.

Running between these pools, the detectives were forced to stop as they heard dozens of footsteps hurrying towards them. Sloan braced himself against a corner wall and peered around the edge. Were they a force of Gabe's men sent to deal with the power outage, or was The Wraith successful? His heart was pounding out of his chest when he saw the shadowy figures of many police officers bounding down the stairs. They did not look to be in armor like the rest of the rebels, so Sloan decided to risk it all and step around the corner.

One of them was armed with an assault rifle, and he pointed it at Sloan while shouting, "Identify yourself!"

Putting his hands up to show cooperation and put the officer at ease, Sloan yelled back, "Detectives Bob Sloan and Rosa Perez. We're on your side!"

"I guess The Wraith managed to save them," Perez said, feeling relieved.

"Well, if that did happen, it was because we turned out the lights in time," Sloan said, unwilling to give a vigilante all the credit for any heroic action that night.

The group of officers descended the stairs discussing the situation. The consensus was that these were two honest cops. "Alright, you are with us." Sloan recognized the officer as Cole.

The detectives exchanged a hasty handshake with Cole, who resumed his questioning with, "We heard sirens. Is there anyone that we can trust on the outside?"

"Yeah, we've got a barricade of cops all around the building." Perez confirmed.

"Right. Here's what's going to happen. We are going to leave the building, get extra weapons from the barricade, and storm the building. The Metro City Police are not going down without a fight!" Cole declared, to the excited agreement of his men.

"What about the Commissioner?" Sloan asked, not seeing him among the men.

"We don't know. He's still in here somewhere; we'll keep our eyes peeled!" Cole vowed.

Having heard enough, Perez stood between Cole and the doorway.

"If you ask me, you're all going off half-cocked. Your plan is to launch a rescue mission, guns blazing, and *hope* not to take out the Commissioner?" Perez challenged the group.

"You and Bob weren't in the building, detective. When they stormed the place, they killed people, good people. I will not risk any more lives by attacking with minimal force. We'll hit them hard and fast, and I guarantee you that we *will not* harm the Commissioner!" Cole said with measured anger.

"You want revenge? So do I, but you have to think it through. We all know that Latham's behind this, and you think that killing potential informants is going to bring him down?" Perez explained.

"What do you suggest? They cleaned out the armory and have high powered assault rifles and body armor. What do you want us to fight back with? Pepper spray? Tazers? Rubber bullets? We'll be massacred!" Cole fought back, and Perez understood his position. There would be no easy victory in this battle.

●●●

The pools of light caused by the power outage were a great aid to The Wraith as he crept through the building. Though he and the Metro City Police were on the same side, they were not allies. In fact, there was a standing order to arrest The Wraith on sight. Thankfully, The Wraith thought, they would be busy contending with their own traitorous team to focus on apprehending him.

The dread avenger had reached the top floor of the building, and hid in the shadows as he heard another man briskly stomping towards the stairs to the roof. The Wraith did not need his night vision to confirm that it was Gabe. His raspy voice could be heard echoing down the corridor as he shouted into his radio.

"This whole damn thing went south! You better be sending the chopper to pick me up, you hear me!" Gabe demanded, looking like he was ready to crush the small device in his hand.

"You are in no position to make demands, officer," was the reply on the radio. The Wraith overheard the voice from his own stolen piece, and recognized it as belonging to Latham. He silently cursed that he had no way to record it for evidence. "You will have to take your chances. I, for one, am not placing my chips on an unsure bet."

"Hey! You can't abandon...!" Gabe screamed, but the harsh static of the radio cut his protest short. Swearing, Gabe put his hands on his hips and took a deep sigh, trying to figure his way out of the situation.

Suddenly, The Wraith pounced upon Gabe, forcing his powerful arms around Gabe's throat and getting him in a choke-hold. Gabe feebly attempted to shoot The Wraith, but his aim was wild and he soon found himself out of bullets. Though The Wraith's grip was strong, Gabe managed to slip out of it and he turned to face the vigilante.

Gabe's eyes went wide with fear as The Wraith's emblem began to glow. The dread avenger advanced on his target, growing more confident in his ability.

"Oh no! I'm not going down that easy!" Gabe yelled. Latham had warned him of The Wraith's infamous Judgment Stare, and the corrupt officer had a strategy. He had managed to avert his gaze. The officer grabbed a small, metal object from his belt and spiked it at the dread avenger.

The Wraith looked down, and instantly recognized it as a grenade! It was not explosive, but rather a flash bang grenade. It was a clever ploy, The Wraith conceded, and he was forced to abandon his Judgment Stare while he covered his eyes with his cape.

The grenade detonated! While The Wraith had spared himself from the blinding flash of white light, he was still victim to the disorienting, high-pitched wail that the weapon emitted. Through he was disoriented and wounded; the dread avenger forced himself to charge at Gabe!

The vigilante collided with Gabe, forcing them both to collapse on the floor of the stairway. The dread avenger managed to climb on top of his opponent, pinning him to the ground. The exertion was agony for The Wraith, who felt the bullet digging deeper into his side with every twist and movement of his body. Gabe was not restricted by this handicap, and swung his fists wildly trying to land a strike. The Wraith's lower jaw was the only unarmored part of his body, and Gabe saw it as a prime target. The Wraith felt blow after blow smash relentlessly into his exposed face.

Gabe then thrust his fist mightily into The Wraith's throat in an attempt to stun his opponent. His armor and cape deflected most of the damage, but The Wraith could tell he was dealing with an experienced fighter. To punish Gabe for his retaliation, the vigilante slugged the corrupt cop with a powerful haymaker.

The punch stunned Gabe and The Wraith closed a vice-like grip around Gabe's throat. "Tell your men to stand down!" The Wraith bellowed while holding the radio to Gabe's face.

With a primal yell, Gabe executed a Jiu-Jitsu technique that freed him from The Wraith's grip. The Wraith was reeling from the pain, and watched as Gabe rolled to his feet.

Gabe began to attack the dread avenger with a series of strong, relentless blows that staggered and battered The Wraith. His kicks had a great deal of force behind them, and Gabe knew to keep his distance from his opponent. The Wraith kept his arms close to his sides and tucked his head in, blocking and diverting Gabe's onslaught of punches and kicks. The Wraith knew the only way to win this fight would be to incapacitate or cripple Gabe, and to do that he would have to get in close. The corrupted cop was clearly not giving him that opportunity.

Any attempt that The Wraith made to reach Gabe aggravated his wound, and he unconsciously winced and contorted. Unfortunately, Gabe witnessed this momentary lapse of control and realized with delight the dread avenger's weak point! He began to pummel The Wraith's wound with a vicious ferocity, and the vigilante felt himself collapsing from the agonizing, unbearable pain.

•••

Cole, Perez, Sloan, and the remaining Metro City Police Officers marched through the front doors of the building. Having pulled weapons from the trunks of the patrol cars, each of them was now equipped with a substantial amount of firepower.

"There has to be a better way," Perez muttered to Sloan.

"I know, but I can't think of any other options!" Sloan said as his finger nervously tapped his assault rifle.

Cole ignored the arguing detectives and addressed the rest of his team, "We've got to play this safe, and I don't want any hero crap! We stay behind cover and move conservatively. We try to take them on in small groups. Everyone got that?"

There was a general muttering of agreement. Their unit was approaching the main lobby when Cole raised his fist. It was a large room, with decorative columns, a built-in reception area, and metal chairs and tables set in groups on the ground floor, with stairs to a second story that overlooked the lobby. Everyone stopped as they heard the flood of footsteps approaching from the upper levels. With rapid hand gestures, Cole silently instructed everyone to find cover. Sloan and Perez hid behind two architectural columns, but he knew that the situation was hopeless. The enemy had the high ground, armor, and superior firepower. All they could hope for was a heroic last stand.

The police watched as their corrupted brethren, all wearing SWAT uniforms, either filed down the stairs or raced out of the elevators. They swarmed around the second story, positioning themselves strategically so they could cover every corner of the downstairs lobby. The SWAT officers cocked their weapons, one after the other, like a perverse orchestra warming up. Cole and his men raised their weapons in defiance.

Each side waited, as if hoping the other would fire first. One could hear a pin drop. Sloan could feel beads of sweat snaking down his skin and he focused his aim on a SWAT officer.

"Wait!" a voice yelled to break the unbearable silence.

•••

The Wraith collapsed onto his back, beaten, bloody, and exhausted. Gabe's assault had almost finished him, but the dread avenger forced himself to keep going. He had managed to inflict substantial damage to his opponent, but Gabe still stood over him. Wiping some blood from the corner of his mouth, Gabe spat on The Wraith, and began to chuckle.

"You know, I ought to thank you. I'll be known as the man who killed The Wraith, and everyone will fear me. Even Latham."

"What you're doing... is wrong," The Wraith spoke, knowing that his words would fall on deaf ears.

"Doesn't feel wrong. Feels pretty damn good actually." Gabe said as he leaned in towards The Wraith, his arrogant face getting closer and closer to the vigilante's head. "You know, for a guy decked out in armor, why would you leave your mouth exposed?"

Menacingly, Gabe raised his steel-toed boot up above The Wraith's head and got ready to stomp down on the dread avenger's jaw. "It doesn't make any..."

Overestimating his own strength, Gabe did not consider that The Wraith was biding his time, like a cobra waiting to strike! The Wraith's hands flew up and seized Gabe's foot, and twisted it with tremendous savagery!

A loud snap, like that of twisting celery, emitted loudly from Gabe's ankle! Gabe screamed in anguish as he feebly attempted to keep his balance. Thinking quickly, The Wraith kicked out and struck the back of his other knee. Another crack of bursting bones filled the hollow stairway. The corrupt officer dropped to the floor, unable to stand.

The Wraith, with tremendous effort, stood over his fallen opponent. The dread avenger removed the stolen radio from his utility belt and forced it up to Gabe's mouth.

"Tell your men to stand down..." The Wraith ordered.

"Wraith, we can work something out. I..." Gabe stammered. He was about to keep on babbling, but he noticed the bright glow that was slowly beginning to radiate from The Wraith's chest emblem. "It's over! You beat me! What are you doing?"

"Cooperate or you face the Judgment Stare."

•••

All eyes were turned on the man who had just entered the lobby. Incredibly, Commissioner George Harrison held no gun, but kept his hands aloft to show that he meant no harm. Cole's men and the SWAT team watched as he strode to the center of the lobby, surveying the scene in front of him. The disgust on Harrison's face was obvious as he shook his head.

"What are we doing here?" he asked. "What was this all about? Injustice? Greed? Revenge? I don't care how any of you try to justify it... wrong is wrong! We are servants of the city, not of ourselves! You think it's a thankless job? Tough! I've been doing it longer than any of you!"

His speech rang throughout the halls, and the SWAT officers began to look at one another. Seeing that they had not lowered their weapons, Harrison cleared his throat and continued.

"Even in a city out to get us, we still had each other! I thought I could look to every one of you and know that you had my back! How wrong I was... you're killing each other, for what? Because a gangster promised you some cash and power? All of you were stupid enough to believe him! What makes you think that a man who built his empire on lies and corruption would honor his deal with you? He is the enemy and now you have become an enemy of Metro City!" Harrison bellowed, and watched as some of the SWAT team lowered their weapons.

A crackle over the radio caught everyone off guard. They heard garbled coughing and a groan, but then the weakened, strained voice of Gabe came through.

"Stand down... that's an order... stand down."

Looking around with uncertainty, the SWAT team did as their leader commanded and placed their firearms on the floor. Harrison motioned to Perez and Sloan.

"They are all under arrest. They know their rights," was his simple command.

"The Wraith did it again," Perez whispered to Sloan as they ascended the staircase with Cole's team.

"And not a moment too soon," Sloan said and cracked a smile for the first time that night.

"No!" Gabe's voice came over the radio again and everyone stopped to listen. He sounded terrified and frantic. "I did as you asked! Let me go! Please, I'll..."

The noise was cut short by the sound of the radio breaking. Sloan and Perez looked to each other, and then to Harrison, as if each had experienced the same eerie chill creep down their spines together.

"Huh," Harrison shrugged, "I wonder what that was all about."

●●●

A bright, golden dawn appeared over Metro City, and the heat was finally beginning to let up. Though he was bruised and tired, Commissioner George Harrison still agreed to appear on the morning news. He expertly fielded the questions from the throngs of reports on the steps outside of police headquarters. The mutinous officers, black bags over their heads, were being shepherded into a military grade prison transport by the trustworthy officers. Harrison thought to spare their families the indignity of being associated with them. The last conspirator loaded onto the transport was Gabe, and he was a shivering, shuddering mess of tears and nerves. He kept manically apologizing and confessing to what he had done, as did most victims of The Wraith's Judgment Stare.

"This is an unprecedented event, Commissioner Harrison. With the police force turning on itself, how can the people of Metro City know who to trust?" a reporter asked, thrusting a microphone in the haggard Commissioner's face.

"It all depends on how you look at it. Yes, this was a shocking and devastating event, but the good people on this police force banded together. I think, if anything, that the police force in Metro City is stronger, and even more united. It was painful to see friend turn against friend, but the worst of the storm has passed." Harrison replied. It was an optimistic turn of events, and did not fully reflect the Commissioner's opinion... but he realized that it was what the people needed to hear.

"Can you confirm reports that the vigilante known as 'The Wraith' was involved in the events?" another reporter asked, her question drowning out all the others.

"I was inside police headquarters the entire time, and I can say with one-hundred percent honesty that I did not see The Wraith. The rebel officers, as you know, knocked out all of the security cameras and recording devices in the building, so it is impossible to verify that The Wraith, if he even exists, was present during these events. As you know, it is the policy of the Metro City Police Department to arrest the vigilante on sight." Harrison confirmed, and his intonation made it clear that this was all he was going to say on the matter.

Robert Latham abruptly switched off the news and turned to face an associate. He was a hefty man, and the unofficial king of Metro City. Latham got up from behind his desk and paced around his opulent, sleek office, hiding his frustration as best as he could. For the moment, all he could mutter was "The Wraith..."

"Yes, sir. I would guess that he *was* involved, despite what the Commissioner says," the associate ventured in an attempt to be helpful.

"Of course he was involved! He's like a cockroach! No matter what I throw at him, he keeps coming back!" Latham said, allowing himself to temporarily lose his calm facade.

"What are we going to do about the conspirators that are currently in custody? There are plenty of them that will confess and implicate you in order to secure their own freedom." Latham's lackey warned. This was acknowledged by a confident scoff from the crime lord.

"Just because our people on the police force have been compromised, does not mean that we have lost control of the situation. I'm sure that some people in our justice department can misplace evidence, attorneys and judges can be bought, and I'll even get a psychiatrist or two to pronounce a few people unfit to stand trail. Failing that... anything can happen in a prison cell. It's tough work keeping an eye on all those inmates, and it would be tragic if a traitor were to be killed before they could get their confession on record." Latham said with mock concern. He leaned back, assuring himself that once again, he had handled the situation with cool efficiency.

"There is also the matter of the officer from internal affairs, Layla Roscoe..."

"Ah, yes. We have failed to get rid of her, and attempting to do so now would only bring suspicion on us. Delete all the necessary files and bury her under legal rhetoric and red tape." Latham said as he waved his hand dismissively in the manner of a Roman emperor.

"And what of The Wraith?" his associate asked while he took notes.

"Him... one day I'll best him. I played my hand and he managed to come out on top. Next time might be different, who knows?" Latham said. He wandered over to a small game table in the corner of his office, where a beautiful marble chessboard stood. The game had come to a strategic standstill; either side would suffer a casualty to gain the upper hand. Latham looked at the white knight, a figure that he had used to symbolize The Wraith. One day, Latham was sure, one day...

The End

ERIK FRANKLIN—is a writer/actor/filmmaker based in Seattle. Graduating with honors from the Art Institute of Seattle in film production, he is the co-President of Franklin-Husser Entertainment LLC. He is working on two upcoming feature films for his company : "Dearly Departed" and "Neo-Criminalus." You can give the company page a "Like" at: https://www.facebook.com/pages/Franklin-Husser-Entertainment-LLC/290795021042906.

Drawn to pulp fiction through his love of history, literature, and Americana, he is grateful for Airship 27 Productions giving him the opportunity to write his first story. He looks forward to writing more adventures!

Sundown
Frank Dirscherl & Adam Oravec

Three. I am The Wraith. Four. Dread Avenger of the Underworld. Five. And that's five less than yesterday. I sit in this cage, as I wince from the pain of the pushups. I look around; I used to be good at measurements, but my mind is hazy, I sometimes have trouble thinking clearly. The cell bars are rusted but still hold true. The floor is concrete and cold on my feet. There is a bed against the left concrete wall, which is mine. My cellmate rests in his bed along the other side. The ceiling is concrete and we have only one window, which is barred on the outside. The cell is not heated but the walls hold off some of the cold of the season. An empty, rusted bookshelf sits in the left corner. A toilet is in front of the window. I massage my arms as I try to remember where I was before I was brought here.

My mind is muddled. Thoughts do not come easily anymore. I can't remember how long I've been here. Sometimes it feels like years. But...I think I've only recently been brought here. I can't quite remember. What I *do* remember, though, is being attacked by members of the Trenchcoat Mafia—the guy's who shot up Columbine years ago. However, they didn't plan this. The Trenchcoat Mafia is too brain-dead to pull something like this off. I am going to remind Trent Remings, their leader, of that as I pound his teeth into his gums. Whoever planned this knew what they were doing and they had patience and timing. They had resources. They were smart and they did their homework. These are professionals.

They have broken my body. Through these bars at night, I see. I see them lock the doors and secure the cells. I see them roam the halls and I see their hands. I hear the keys jingle in their pockets. They have broken my body, but I try to keep my mind as clear and focused as possible, but I often find it hard to remember the past. It all seems...muzzy somehow. But I am patient; pretty soon there will be no need for bruises, blood, or broken glass. I will just slip out of here. I will simply no longer exist in this place.

I feel a pain in my lower back as I try to stand. I press my hand against my bed to gain leverage as I try to balance myself. I get up off the floor. My clothes are wet with sweat and I am tired, but I am able to move. I use whatever I can to make my way toward the window. Each step of my right foot sends shockwaves to my lower back. I see the light of the moon shining through the window. I reach out for it. I place my hand against the chilled glass. My sweaty fingertips begin to freeze against it.

I look out at the moonlit city. Metro City, my home. I miss the rooftops, the streets and the alleyways. Especially the alleyways. Once again, the city will be mine. One day. I remove my hand from the glass. I look down at it as I rub my fingers together in order to rub out the cold. What I miss most of all, however, is...

I hear a burst. I turn to my cellmate. He lies in the fetal position with his back turned toward me. His white prison pants slowly turn yellowish green as they absorb the diarrhea. Further down his pants, streaks appear as the mess runs down the back of his legs. I make my way back to my bed.

• • •

The weather was bitterly cold as I held firm to the building's ledge, but my costume protected me from the brunt of it. I blessed Max for his eternal ingenuity.

The Black Guerrilla family had just raped and tortured three members of the Mexican Mafia and their families. Tensions were high. Scum didn't wash clean in the middle of the Christmas season. Music was playing from the accompanying building. I forgot the song but it provided no comfort. I sat perched as I watched a TV and computer repair store opposite—a drug front belonging to the Black Guerrilla family. If there was going to be a reprisal, this was a likely place. And, one of my best snitches told me tonight was the night.

I waited for three hours wishing I was somewhere warm with Leena. I still hadn't bought her that scarf she wanted. Then, it happened. *She* happened. The first thing I noticed was the eggshell white wool knitted cap, her hair streaming out of the back. She was a brunette, her nose was narrow and her lips full. My heart popped with each step she took. She was wearing a white jacket and white gloves. Her pants were a different shade of the same color. Her boots were black, high heels.

She carried two bags, one in each hand. They were those big department store bags with the store's name in big bold letters on each side. She walked up to the shop, turned and faced it. The Family loves their white women but something was wrong there. She was far from the kind of trash that fell for them. Not their style. I leaned forward as she kicked on the front door. The door opened and she walked in. Another followed, a man, but...I could't see him clearly. It's as though, he existed in a haze. And yet...

•••

I wake, my dreams making little sense to me. My pillow is soaked and smells like a wet dog. I notice that my bed covers are on the ground. I must have gotten hot last night. I begin to get up and then get dizzy. Sitting up in bed all hunched over, I need to catch my breath. Picking up the covers, I stand up to shake them out. Dust and a few cockroaches fall from them. I try to stomp on the roaches but they are too fast, as they scurry toward the drain in the middle of the floor. I fold my covers and place them on my bed. I turn around and look over to my cellmate. He still lies there in the same position. The diarrhea which now covers the bed sheets and the mattress is dry. The room is starting to stink. Despite this, I am starting to get hungry for breakfast. I turn to my cell doors as I hear the guards' footsteps.

With each guard on either side of me, I make my way through the dingy concrete hallway, shackled. I figure that starting a fight in my cell wouldn't help matters. I need to escape and not spend the rest of my time in solitary confinement. The hallway is empty. Lights hang from the ceiling. There are no windows. The guards say nothing as they hurry me through a side door.

I enter the cafeteria still under special escort. The guards undo my shackles but keep a hold of me. My nose begins to sting. The place smells like strong bleach. I almost slide on the slick white tile floors. The guards tighten their grip around my arms and pull me up slightly. They then push me along my way and into the back of the line. I pick my head up and notice that I am not alone.

Housed in this foul, stinking excuse of a cafeteria is a collection of Metro City's worst. Old mob bosses, former drug dealers, runaway skinheads, and other assorted trash eat slop and converse about their newfound luck. Not one person stops what they are doing, not one person picks their head up to see me being dragged into this delightful place. They don't know my identity.

I make my way to the buffet containing the plastic utensils and paper plates. I pick one of each up and continue on my way. The plate is barely sturdy enough to hold the pancake-like sludge that the cooks throw on them. I come out into the sitting room and I sit by myself in the back. I pull up my sleeves and pick up my knife and fork, ready to spend a half hour trying to mop up my meal.

I hear a shuffling noise and I look up. An elderly man approaches me, his hair wiry and grey, his skin mottled and brown. Carrying his plate in front of his waist, he sits down. He hunches over his plate and shovels the food in his mouth. He chews and then wipes his mouth with his sleeve. Portions of pancake and toast become smeared on it. I briefly watch this disgusting display. He stops and motions his head toward a woman sitting by herself.

"The Maguire boy got to her again last night. Smashed that hammer on nail."

I look at him as he continues to shovel food in his mouth. He grabs another slice of toast and slops up the remnants of his pancakes. I look back at the woman.

In time, the guards take me back to my cell. The smell of bleach is rampant and further irritates my nose. I notice my cellmate is now gone. His sheets and pillow are gone. I notice some stains on his bed. Crouching down, I inspect them closely. Some stains are brown and yellow, probably the diarrhea, and are consistent and in no specific pattern. They had some trouble picking him up. I observe some bloodstains, but can't tell if they beat him, if there was some blood in his stool, or if the stains are older. A slight chill goes down my spine. I believe he is dead.

Later on, I find myself in the activity room. It reeks of bleach and old baby diapers. The room has no windows but a smattering of overhead lights provide a lot of illumination. I crouch up against the corner wall, with my back facing the prison guards. A man, whom I don't recognize, comes toward me. He moves slow and stops in front of me. I don't look him in the eye. I keep my focus at his feet.

"You a new one here, ain't cha'?" he said.

I just nod my head and keep my focus on his feet. He decides to crouch down next to me. He looks me in the eye as I shyly glance at his face and look away again. He gets too close for comfort.

"Welcome to Hell, boy."

I don't acknowledge him. I just keep my eyes focused away from him and onto one spot in the room. He begins to shake as if he suffers from Parkinson's Disease.

"I bet you wonderin' why everything smells like bleach in here."

I look into his eyes. They're a piercing blue in shade. His face looks older than it should, but there's still a brightness there to indicate this place hasn't fully gotten to him yet. He moves his head closer.

"It's a toxin. Some type of protein blocker."

I don't move my eyes.

"How long have you been here, son?"

I mumble incoherently. He smiles.

"And I bet you're wonderin' how come you ain't got to taste cooked meat."

I look away as he moves his head closer.

"Name's Mattie," he says, before continuing with his explanations. "They got us on a vegetarian diet. They're makin' us weak. Breaking down our muscles, till there is no chance of escape."

I shuffle.

"So when you get a chance to fight the system, hell, it's worth a shot... huh?" He arches an eyebrow at me.

He reaches inside his tattered jacket and into his shirt pocket. He looks back at the guards and then shuffles me further into the corner. He is now in front of me. He pulls out a bag of bug parts. Cockroach legs, a beetle's thorax, and other assorted body parts rest inside the bag. He pulls the bag apart and it opens. Surprisingly, or maybe not, it doesn't stink. He looks at me.

"Go on now, get a taste."

I stare at him as I reach into the moist bag. I grab something hard, maybe a leg. I pull it out of the bag and without looking at it, without thinking, I stick it in my mouth. It feels like a spiny twig in my mouth, but maybe a little softer. He smiles as I chew it. He then closes the bag. He puts it back into his shirt pocket, and looks over at the guards and then towards another inmate.

"Ms. Laura is looking at you," he says.

I follow his eyes, and see an old wheelchair bound woman staring at me. She motions for me to come over. The man—Mattie—gets up and leaves and I make it to my feet, which are now killing me. I hobble over towards the woman in the chair.

I stand awkwardly in front of her as she motions for me to bend down. I do so and she lifts herself a little in her chair.

"Looks like you got a broom," she said. "Want to do some spring cleaning?"

She slaps me in the crotch and starts laughing. Her breath stinks and she doesn't have all of her teeth.

Once I'm back in my cell, I start to go to work on my bed. I grab the end of it and flip it over. Then, I grab the left leg and start twisting and turning it, trying to rip it off. I start to bang on my walls, trying to find a weak spot. I grab around the base of my toilet and pull on it, trying to rip it out of the floor.

I grip the back lid of the toilet and hurl it at the glass window. The glass breaks and I throw my arms around the bars. The sharp edges of the shattered glass cut my arms a little, but I can reach the bars. I yank on the bars trying to rip them out of place. In the end, I just wear myself out. In the late afternoon I sit on the concrete floor, with my sore back, up against my turned over bed. I am holding my right shoulder, which I think I strained when I was pulling on the toilet. Am I ever going to get out of here? I try hard not to let a sense of defeat and despair overwhelm me.

After all...tomorrow is another day.

• • •

Outside at night they have us walking in a straight line, down a covered concrete hallway. The sides of the hallway are open, except at one point where a wall of the main building runs adjacent to it. Trash cans line that section of wall. I make a mental note to try and find out whose cell is in that area of the building. The cold wind freezes my extremities. They are trying to boost morale in the prison by having bingo night. I look down at the ground and notice them. Discs, embedded in the dirt, barely noticeable...but I can see them. They are spaced out evenly, all the way up to the fence line. Too many to just water the lawn. I notice a small space at the base of the wire fence almost directly opposite me in the distance, almost like a gap. Too small for a man, but...

Later, when I'm sitting in the activity hall, playing bingo with the rest of the group, I can't get my mind off those discs. I don't hear the person rattling off the number and letter combinations. I am not entirely sure if I know *how* to play bingo. However, it seems that the person next to me is focused and happy playing my card. I am done here. I raise my hand in order to get the attention of the guards. A portly specimen comes up beside me and leans down.

I am walking down the same hallway as several guards pass me by. After apologizing for the damage done to my cell and promising to 'never do it again,' I've been good the last couple weeks. I am no longer shackled, having been rewarded for my good behavior. I walk slowly out into the yard and investigate the discs. I must have not been paying attention to where I was going. I stumble, hitting the concrete hard, my brain jostling in my skull. I sit and stare at one of the discs as the pounding in my head slowly subsides. The disc is wet and has dirt on the top and the sides. I glance up at the towers. There are no spotlights out tonight. I realize—to reach the gap in the fence, you would have to traverse the dusty ground covered with the discs. I focus my attention back to the disc before me. It blinks, however, there doesn't seem to be any invisible lasers being emitted from it. I press at a spot on the top. Nothing happens. I get up, stumble a bit, and continue on my way.

Making my way back into the main building, I walk into the containment area and pass several cells. Many of the cells here are like mine. Some prisoners here have more privileges than others...no doubt a reward for kissing butt. Some prisoners have better bookshelves. Others have closets to place their clothes, some TV's and videogames. As I begin to walk past a cell, I hear someone whisper.

I look into the cell and see a bed, being illuminated by a near-full moon that shines through the window, which is against the right side wall. Old ragged sheets cover the bed in full. At the head of the bed, I see fingers sticking up from under the covers. I see the shape of a head peeking out, two eyes emerging slowly. They stare at me and then stare straight ahead. A hand comes out from under the covers and points to something ahead.

I walk into the room and right up to the side of the bed. The woman doesn't turn to me but keeps her eyes focused straight ahead.

"There's a werewolf in my closet," she mumbles.

I turn and look straight ahead. The closet sits closed and, like the gates of Heaven, is illuminated. There are no noises coming from it. However, I approach it slowly. A broom rests against the wall next to the closet and I grab it for insurance. The woman whispers inaudibly as she still rests in her bed. I slowly grab for the handle and pull the closet door open.

"There it is!" she screams. Nothing. "Get it!" she screams again.

I swing wildly at nothing.

"Kill it!"

I spend the next five minutes beating up air as the woman cheers me on.

Later, after having vanquished the monster, Mattie, the bug man from the activity center, and I hang out in my cell catching cockroaches. He crouches down and inspects the base of the reinserted toilet as I spend my time hunched around the bookshelf. He teaches me the finer arts of capturing the more meaty ones.

"You know what part of the cockroach has the most protein in it? It's the guts. Most people squash 'em, but they're just taking out the best parts. You gots to give 'em one good smacks, that's all it takes. They ain't like ticks where you got to give them your Ike Turner, just a little smacks will do. You taste what I'm slinging?"

I give out an agreeable moan. My mind is more focused on the werewolf expedition I had earlier. I have been debating on whether to bring it up with Mattie or not. I decide to speak up.

"I ran into a woman earlier. She asked me to kill a werewolf in her closet."

He stops and looks up at me. "Mary Martha. You kill it?"

I sit up on my knees and stare at the ground in front of me. "It wasn't there."

He smiles. "Man, I know that. They been injecting her with Haloperidol."

I know of it. Mattie continues.

"Haloperidol causes depression. One of the symptoms of depression is hallucination."

I look at the old man. "How do you know?"

He gives the answer so clearly. "This place is a prison, after all."

He has to be right. It's the only logical conclusion. Is this why my own mind is so muddled at times?

"You know what that is son? Haloperidol?"

I nod.

"The Soviets used it to break the will of their prisoners."

I look away. "That has to be it."

Mattie becomes excited. "What does?"

I shuffle. "Whoever is doing this is kidnapping old time mobsters and criminals...ones that are retired...have been cast out, or were previously incarcerated. If they're kidnapped, no-one is going to come looking for them. Little to no people will care. Whoever's behind this are injecting these criminals with Haloperidol in order to gain access to information. And information means money."

The old man squints. "You a detective or something?"

I nod. "Something like that. But why kidnap me? I have people who will come looking for me. Why risk getting caught?"

The old man points a crooked finger at me and I turn and look at him, already knowing the answer.

"Maybe you were on to them. Maybe they needed you out of their way for just a little bit. Just for a little bit, then it wouldn't matter if someone finds you because it would be complete. Their final plan."

That's it. It must be, I think.

"What is their final plan then?"

The old man shakes his head. "You're the detective."

The rest of the morning, Mattie and I catch bugs and talk.

• • •

I heard gunshots, so I quickly used my grapnel and line and lowered myself to the ground. Upon entering the store, I slipped on an intestine and instantly noticed the blood soaked floor. Chunks of body parts lay scattered everywhere.

I looked up past the human flotsam. Her black boots appeared even darker with red tints on them. Chunks of flesh hung from the part where the boot met the pant leg, almost if they had been placed there with care. Her white pants were now a bright pink, the blood discoloring them intensely. But where was the other one? The man. Did he even exist?

Her coat was gone and her white shirt was torn as blood covered the clothes and her flesh as it appeared out of the cuts in her top. Her ample breasts showed evidence of her excitement. Her porcelain nose was now sprayed red with blood along with the lower part of her face. Her eyes were green. The white wool knit cap was now gone, her hair flowed in the breeze from the open door. Her brunette hair was flecked with streaks of blood.

She had begun to saw into his neck when I burst in. He no doubt died instantly, but in her insanity, she was determined to take off the head. His body was limp. Blood squirted each time she dug deeper into the hapless victim's flesh. I couldn't keep my eyes off her. I watched her as she completed the decapitation. The body fell and the head followed with it. She just stared at me with a hatchet in one hand, the other hand clenched in an awful rage. She stood there, staring at me, like a deer caught in a car's headlights. I took a moment before regaining my composure.

"Stay where you are!" I demanded.

She continued to breathe heavily as if she was shocked that I said that. "Catch me."

She threw the hatchet at me, but I managed to evade it in time. It would have split my head in two. She took off, hurdling furniture and body parts, surprisingly agile in those high heels. Quickly, she headed toward a window, crashed through it, and I made to follow. She was already off and running by the time I landed. Was someone else running away? The man? As I got my bearings, she was sprinting down the sidewalk. I began

"CATCH ME."

to pick up speed, but she was fast, deceptively so. People screamed and fell to the ground as she careened into them. I managed to avoid them as I continued my chase.

Up ahead, she crashed into a large man, which bought me enough time to catch up. Upon my urging, he grabbed her by the arms but by the time I got there, she had kneed him in the groin and was off again. This time she cut out into the traffic. Drivers blasted their horns and stepped on their brakes. She darted in-between them like a graceful ballerina. I followed quickly but was less fortunate, being side-swiped by an S.U.V.

I didn't allow that to slow me, and continued my pursuit. We rounded a corner and I caught sight of her ducking into a shadowy alleyway. It started to snow as she jumped the wall at the far end. I did likewise and we continued thus, through a succession of streets and narrow alleys, her agility and stamina astounding me.

Eventually, we came into Hyde Park. Snow drifts were building, and her footprints proved easy to follow. The moon was full and the surrounding trees cast eerie shadows around us. Finally, the deep snow began to slow her down. I jumped her by the lake, the snow stinging my face. In the moonlight, I saw just how beautiful she was.

I lay on top of her, as she fought like a hellcat, smashing her fists into my shoulders and chest. Her legs were going nowhere as I loomed over her. I forced my weight upon her as she continued to struggle as best she could. The Eyes of Judgment began to glow on my chest.

"You who have sinned against humanity, now is your time of judgment. Repent!"

Her struggling slowly ceased and eventually stopped as she glared into the Eyes. She paused.

And then started laughing.

• • •

I spend the early morning watching the people out in the prison yard. I am comfortable like this, watching people from a distance. It seems that I can see everything from here, people conversing in the center. Further up in the yard, guards occupy several buildings. Below, past some tape and fencing, guards are working on a drainpipe. I notice a dog making its way across the yard—a German Shepherd—wagging its tail as it holds a branch in its mouth. It makes its way up to its owner. He grabs the dog's cheeks in approval. He looks familiar to me, but I cannot place him.

Days after the incident in the yard, I find the cell of Brownstown Bob. He is absent but I know that it is his. Books from the prison library are littered throughout. All of them are about dogs, the only thing he has ever loved in this world. Mattie told me about him, told me he was here, and it was then that I remembered him. And just my luck, his cell is in the section of the building alongside the outer covered walkway, close to the gap in the fence. I knew then that he's my one hope of escape.

In the old days, he ran a dog rescue facility. It was a front for his burglary business. He would train the dogs to break into people's houses and retrieve goods. Every penny went to the dogs—they were treated like kings while he lived in filth. We would have never caught him if it weren't for his old Bess. The dog was old and forgetful, but even in her old age she was still the best. Or so Bob thought. She had gone in to retrieve some priceless jewelry from a gunrunner's house. The intended victim couldn't sleep that night, and was preparing a snack in the kitchen. She would have gotten past him, if she would have remembered what she was there for. A sucker for Swiss cheese, she walked right up to him. She startled him and he shot her. Hearing the gun go off, Bob, who was parked near the scene, grabbed a lead baseball bat and burst in. Seeing his dog dead on the floor, he took a bullet in the shoulder, then shattered the gunrunner's kneecaps. In his fury, he then proceeded to shatter the rest of him.

I wake up early so that the guards know that I am ready for breakfast. I want to catch Brownstown in the cafeteria and talk with him. Unfortunately, the guards don't arrive until late. Once again, I am last in line and have to wait for an eternity to get my sloppy pancakes. I make it out into the sitting area and I notice Brownstown sitting with fellow inmates. He's nearly finished his breakfast. I walk over to him.

"Hey, Brownstown," I call.

He lifts his head. I come up behind a fellow inmate, who sits in front of Brownstown.

"Brownstown. We need to talk."

Brownstown motions his head toward the left and he gets up. I follow. We walk toward a corner of the cafeteria. He becomes nervous.

"I saw you with that German Shepard."

He steps back. "Oh man, don't tell no one."

Tell them what? "I...I don't know what you mean."

He looks a little panicked. "That I been using her to...steal stuff."

I shake my head. "I'm not telling anyone, Bob, it's ok."

I pull him further away from everyone else. "I want out of here."

He says nothing.

"Maintenance is working on a drainpipe on the south end."

He steps back.

"They are bound to have blueprints with them. All I want is the landscape, that is all I want to know."

He shakes his head. "I can't. I only did some little things so far, nothing big. If they find out I started again, that I helped you."

"Nobody is going to find out, Bob," I said. "Dog goes in, gets blueprints. I look them over, and she puts them back. No one finds out."

"What's in it for me?" he asks after a moment of thought.

I step closer to him to whisper. "How long has it been, Bob, since you've seen her."

He tears up.

"Since you put flowers on her grave."

He wipes his mouth as he nods. He agrees to help me there and then.

Over the next few days during breakfast, Bob and I discuss his training sessions with the dog. In his former life, he was a criminal. Now Bob is an asset. And he's found a kindred spirit in Martha, an eight-year-old German Shepherd. I can use them both to my advantage. We walk together along the cafeteria wall.

"The blueprints stay in an old tool shed, they are never brought out, they don't want people to see them," Bob whispers. "If you pay attention, you know that they are there."

I lower my head. "Where does Martha come in?"

He looks to the side as he takes heavy breathes. "The shed is locked up every afternoon at five."

I look at some guards mulling around. "I noticed something."

He nods. "The discs?"

I nod back.

He continues. "They come up about eight. If we get Martha in and out before then, it shouldn't be a problem. We study the blueprints at night, then return them at five in the morning when the discs go back into the ground, just before the guards are at the towers."

I smile. He's getting into this. "You think she's up to it?"

"She's amateur at best. I was able to steal a section of blueprint paper from the library once. But that was sometime ago and these are old and have picked up the stench of different people throughout the years." He lowers his head as he sticks his hands in his pockets. "It would be a miracle if she gets them."

I smile. "Luckily for the both of us, I happen to believe in miracles."

●●●

There was no sign in the sky and there were very few random meetings on rooftops. Everything was scheduled and everything was by the book. Not because I wanted it that way but because it *had* to be that way. Our meetings often occurred in the park. He once told me it allowed him to clear his head. But I think he really missed Colorado. Commissioner Harrison never let anyone really know how strong or smart he was.

I always assumed that it would have just given him more headaches. I tried not to make him mad. I tried not to let him see my face; even with the mask, he might have figured it out. So I stayed back in the shadows. I didn't often have to announce myself; somehow he usually knew that I was there. But he never knew when I had gone.

He always tolerated me, gave me mostly free reign to do what I had to do...what he couldn't do. I never took that for granted and somehow I never thanked him. He stood on a bridge, which covered a frozen stream. His warm breath came out like smoke and it looked like he hadn't shaved in days. He was hunched over the edge of the bridge, spitting tobacco fragments into the frozen water.

"Some Family members got chopped up last week. We found two small hatchets," Harrison muttered. "One stuck in a wall next to the door. The other one stuck up a man's butt. We found some woman's clothing, a knitted cap in particular. There were some hair fibers in it. We ran those through our system. Nothing. Now Interpol's giving us a headache over this. Apparently some assassins escaped their clutches and made their way here. We think it was them. You don't know anything about that do you?"

He knew that I did. "She escaped me."

"We have witnesses that saw you chase them down a multitude of streets," Harrison said firmly. "And one of them into the park."

He doubted my story. "She got away."

"I don't understand how that could be possible. Once you have someone in your thrall with those...Eyes of yours."

He didn't understand. How could he?

"Don't you hear me? They've slaughtered hundreds of people, in Europe and now they're here in my town!"

He didn't understand...that I loved her.

• • •

The miracle has happened. In my cell trying to get some rest, I suddenly feel Martha's wet nose on my back. I turn around and she sits there staring at me. Bob is behind her wearing a big smile. I look up at him. We move over to his cell. He points at the table and goes under his bed. I keep watch as he pulls out the blueprints.

"Clear off that table."

I retire from my watch as I wipe off junk from his table and he lays the blueprints down. He spreads them open.

"There she is."

I point to several dots on the blueprints. "There are the discs."

He nods.

"I wonder how much weight they can handle?"

He points below the discs. "What's this?"

Bad news. A grid comprised of lasers below the discs, making the act of digging under to escape virtually impossible. The stuff was everywhere. Bob rolls up the blueprints. He looks at me.

"I'm sorry," he says.

Later, feeling deflated, I once again find myself doing the penguin toward the cafeteria, waiting in line for whatever swill they're calling dinner tonight, which is now set up like a cheap high school prom. Several new 'residents' have been brought to the prison and they are having an orientation dance. I find myself staring outside.

How much weight can those discs handle? I think. *They're set to go off when a prisoner steps on them. I'm sure squirrels and raccoons walk all over these at night and I haven't heard them go off once.*

I decide there and then that I need to get my hands on one. I need to touch it, open it up, find out more about them.

I sit by myself in the cafeteria as I watch everybody dance. Right now I can't keep my mind off of Martha, as I don't see Bob embarrassing himself on the dance floor. I really have to get out of here. I begin to get up and feel a pain in my back. An elderly woman comes up to me.

"Hey, stud, want to dance?"

I don't have time for this. "Some other time."

I smile. It's fake.

She points to my chair and I sit. She sits down next to me.

"Margaret. My name is Margaret."

She looks at me as if expecting a response. That name doesn't sound familiar, so I don't respond. She looks back at everyone as they dance. I stare at them. She smiles, looks back at me as I continue to stare.

"When did they get you?"

She might have some clues about my kidnapping. I decide to risk it. "I was kidnapped," I say, not really answering her question.

This peaks her interest. "Kidnapped? By whom?"

I look down at my feet. "Whoever runs this place. They hired the Trenchcoat Mafia to do the job."

She looks confused. "Trenchcoat Mafia, you say? Never heard of them."

She's lying. They've been in the papers since the Columbine school shooting. They're a prominent gang of street toughs. I decide to interrogate her some more. "Who put you in here?"

"Woke up one morning, saw some people in my house. They grabbed me up, tossed me in a van. No trench coats, though."

I shake my head. I start to get up. "The warden is working for someone else, someone who's planning something big. I'm going to find out who."

I leave her and move out into the yard. It's nice to not be surrounded by guards twenty-four-seven anymore. It's just starting to get dark. Everyone is back at the dance. Checking to see if I'm being watched, I start to pull on one of the discs, from the bottom up. My strength isn't what it was but I should be able to pull this out. I pull hard and my fingers are hurting as the disc cuts into them. I can feel my lower back pull. I have my teeth down on my lower lip, giving it everything I have. I can hear pops and fizzles as the wiring pulls away from the base. I pull it until it comes out. I stand up, very sore, and put it in my pocket. I kick some dirt over the top of the exposed wiring of the base. I look to see if anyone noticed. Once I convince myself that no one has, I make my way back to my cell.

Walking there, I hear the distinct sounds of a struggle. A cell door rests open and I peer inside. The moonlight coming in from the tiny window beside the bed illuminates the room. The Maguire boy's back faces me. He is on top of a bed hunched over his latest victim. He holds her down on the bed as I come up behind him. His arms hold hers above her head. He is not forceful with his weight, and it doesn't take much to hold her down.

She is wearing a pink and white blouse and her body contains no visible signs of injury. She looks past him and right at me, though he doesn't notice. He is too busy sizing her up, admiring her. Her eyes are watery. She's been crying, but she doesn't scream out.

Her mascara is smudged all over her face. He takes his hands off her wrists but she doesn't fight back, she would never have a chance if he started pounding on her face. She keeps her arms above her head. He straightens up and places his hands on her chest. He begins to undo her blouse. I decide to speak up.

"Let her go, son."

He turns his upper body toward me. Her hands stretch out toward his face in a failed attempt to scratch his eyes out.

"Go back to your room and leave her alone," I demand.

He ignores me, turns back to his victim. He continues to work the buttons on her blouse. I look down and to my left. There is a wooden broom up against the wall. I pick it up. With everything I have, I snap it in half and before he can turn around, I have it up over my head. He turns around and just stares, sweat pouring off his forehead.

His shirt is covered in various sweat stains of different size and color. He sits there with his mouth open. He slobbers like a dog with a blank expression. A fat slob of a man that rapes old women. I bring the broom down onto the top of his nose, hard. A sharp cracking is heard. I snapped it clean through. Strangely, he doesn't make a sound. Small droplets of blood begin to trickle out of his nose. Then as he touches it, it begins to gush.

I bring the broom back up and into the side of his face. He spits blood and his head jerks to the side. He falls off of the bed. I make my way round before he can get up. He is up on one knee and blood gushes from his nose and starts trickling out of the corner of his mouth. I put everything I have into this one. I swing into his face with all my strength.

I hear the crack and I feel the broom break his teeth. He falls down again. A few more swings. He opens his mouth to scream, but nothing comes. Blood just pours out of the bottom of his mouth. After a few more moments of this, I kick strongly into his crotch, ending it. I throw the broom down and leave.

I limp my way into my cell. My back, shoulders, and arms ache intensely. I am out of breath and soaked with sweat. I shouldn't be this exhausted, this out of shape. Despite this, I am on top of the world. Elated. I look over toward my roommate's bed. I make my way toward my own. If I could jump on it I would. I reach into my pocket and pull out the disc.

I throw it in between my mattress pads. I lie in bed and curl up in the fetal position. I breathe heavily and feel a little cold, but I throw what little covers I have over me and bury my sweaty head into my pillow.

For the first time in a long time, I feel important. I've done some good here. Things are going to change.

I can feel it.

• • •

The morning comes and I wake. My body hurts. As I try to roll over, I realize I'm so stiff I can barely move. The bed stinks of body odor and urine. I must have slept through the night and messed myself. Two guards come by my room. One of them stops and sees my face.

"You okay?" he asks.

Now is not the time for pride. Those days are long gone.

"I messed myself," I reply.

He turns toward the other one. They unlock my cell and enter. They help me to my feet.

The washrooms are clean enough. They have that fake tile on the floors, sinks, and shower cubicles. The only noticeable grime is found in the cracks of the tiles and those around the sole bathtub, which is starting to turn a yellowish color from the water. Pictures of a variety of beach scenes cover the walls. My favorite one is of the lighthouse. It must be a finger-painting or something. It is different from the others. I stand in the shower, in the lukewarm water as Andy and Marcus watch me bathe.

I try telling them that I am capable of doing this myself, but they know I am not allowed. Not after Peggy Burmstine dug into the soap with her fingernails and stuck her own neck. It took them three weeks to clean that washroom. As I begin to wash my crotch, Andy decides to lighten things up. I don't look them in the eye.

"Damn dude, the girls must have loved you."

Marcus chuckles. I don't let them get to me.

"Look at his face, he knows it, he knows it's true," Marcus says.

They both burst out in laughter. Scum.

Afterwards, I make my way into the cafeteria and tensions are high. There are people running, talking, and generally glaring at one another. I get my pancake slop and make my way through the line in a daze. I try not to make eye contact, but I am starting to feel that everyone knows the truth. If accusations are made here, I will not be able to escape.

For the first time in this place, I'm scared. I assume my regular position in the back of the cafeteria. I keep my head down and focused on my meal. A man, whom I believe to be the warden, judging by his dress and demeanor, approaches me with three others from the front. I don't turn around but continue to eat.

"You gonna tell me where you were last night?" the warden queries.

I don't have to be afraid of him. I don't have anything to say to him. I look up and stare straight ahead, as though I'm looking through him.

"I don't have to say anything to you," I say blankly but firmly.

"That's right. You don't have to say anything." He starts to sit beside me as he points to the chair. "This seat taken?"

I shrug. He sits down anyway. He faces me and clasps his hands together. "Several people said they saw you leave the party early."

I continue to spoon the soggy slush into my mouth. He looks up at one of his cohorts and then looks back at me.

"One of our guys got hurt last night. You wouldn't know anything about that would you?"

I detect some menace in his voice, but I don't know what he is talking about. Maguire's not one of them. With my mouth full of pancakes, I tell him that I don't know anything. "Must have had an accident, these things happen a lot here you know. People fall, people walk into doors."

He nods his head and begins to get up. "People beat others with broom handles."

I glance at him out of the corner of my eye. I feel really confused at this point.

He stands to my side as the others remain at my back. "We are done here. But if we find out that you did anything to Mike, it's over."

I continue to eat.

Later, shrugging my encounter with the warden off, I am in the activity room, crouched in a corner. I pull the disc out of my pocket and flip it through my hands a couple of times. I look back at the guards who are not paying attention. I try to find a spot where I can open it up. Then I find it, a little tab at the top of the disc.

Opening it, I find a small network of wirings. Inside the lid, I find a label. It tells me that the disc will go off if pressure exceeds one hundred pounds. I look up from the disc and stare straight ahead. A small smirk comes to my face. Mattie approaches.

"What you got there, detective?"

Luckily it is low enough for the guards not to notice. I don't even look at him. "My way out."

The next morning, I eat breakfast in a hurry. I will probably get indigestion, but it's worth it. I can't wait to tell Bob about my plan. I enter his cell as he sits at his desk and reads. His back is facing me but I can tell he knows that I am there.

"Sounds like you created quite a scene," he says.

Ignoring him, I walk in and sit on his bed. The mattress is old and has some give to it. And it smells.

"I've got a plan."

OPENING THE DISC, I FIND A SMALL NETWORK OF WIRINGS.

He continues to read. I don't think he wants to hear any of it. "We can't dig underground and we don't know what kind of pressure those sensors can handle," Bob says.

I smile. "One hundred pounds."

He closes the book and looks at me like a schoolteacher scolding a student. I throw him the disc I stole earlier.

"I took it from the yard, during the dance."

He studies the disc. "So we know that it will go off on one hundred pounds or more of constant pressure. A lot of good it does us. We both weigh more than that."

I smile. "Except *we* won't be doing the walking."

He looks concerned, but understands quickly. "So we are going to have Martha do it? Tiptoe around the yard? What is she going to do?"

"Get word out."

He begins to stand up. "Get word to who? Everyone I know and care about is dead."

I stand up as well and my back still hurts. "I have a fiancée. Leena. If Martha can get a note to her."

He picks up his book and holds it close to his chest. He chuckles sardonically. "Okay, okay. So Martha is going to make her way across the yard, dig under the fence, travel who knows how long to Metro City, and find one girl in a sea of millions of people?"

I fold my arms. It sounded better in my head.

"Yes," I say determinedly. "But she won't have to dig under the fence. There's a small gap there she can squeeze through."

He puts his book back on the bookshelf. He braces himself against it. His back is toward me. "Then tell me, how are we going to do this...just take her out in the yard? Guards watch that fence all day and night."

I walk over to his far wall. "Your cell runs right alongside the covered walkway outside. We dig a hole in the floor leading to the outside walkway. And the spotlights aren't on that section of the fence all night. It'll be easy for Martha to run there and squeeze through without anyone noticing."

I stomp on the floor. He turns toward me.

"So now we have a huge doggy tunnel through our floor and no one is going to walk by and notice it? What about outside? You're crazy!"

I continue to stomp, smiling as I do so. "We cap off both ends. We use the bookshelf to further conceal it in here, and flush the dirt and dust down the toilet. The outside cap we can hide with the trash cans lining the wall there. They're full of water, used for watering the gardens and never moved."

He faces me straight on and folds his arms. He's not sure. "Even if we could make it work, she would still have to find your Leena in a city the size of Metro. It's not possible." He rubs his chin in thought. I can practically see the wheels of his brain churning. Some seconds later, a small smile creeps onto his features. "Still, I don't see why we can't complete the tunnel and get Martha out there undetected, as you say. She's roughly eighty some pounds...so the sensors shouldn't go off."

He's buying into it.

"Sounds like a plan?" I ask enthusiastically.

He nods his head. "More like suicide." He sighs. "All right. I'm in. I still think its crazy, but it's the best plan anyone here's ever had. Anything's better than staying another minute in this place."

"Good," I say, gripping his shoulders, grateful to have his continued help.

"We get some equipment from the tool shed. Nothing big, or it'll be noticed," he continues. "A couple of months, maybe, and then it will take a while to get her trained."

I begin to leave. "All we have is time."

After that conversation, I have a new energy, feel a new strength flooding my limbs. This place isn't going to beat me. Soon, I will be free, reunited with Leena and Max, back home at last. And those responsible for my imprisonment here will pay. Oh yes, they'll pay dearly.

Over the next few weeks we work on the floor. Martha would steal certain tools—hammers, a chisel and some screwdrivers—from the supply shed (as she is faster and harder to spot in the dark) when we need them and return them, without anyone being the wiser. Bob and I determined to remain on our best behavior so as not to arouse any suspicions. I am less watched, over time, as a result. Our lives pretty much remain the same. A new cellmate would come join me, then disappear. Bob always is alone. One of the terms of his imprisonment.

My mind remains focused on escape, though still hazy on other details. My body, however, is wasting away. Even though my weight remains largely the same, I am losing muscle mass. I try supplementing my diet with the filthy creatures Mattie introduced me to, but it's not enough. I tire easily now.

We share the digging as best we can. Our plan is simple. We try not to see each other besides when we meet up to dig. We have two schedules that we switch over every other month so that the guards won't get suspicious. If anyone had caught us they would think that we were two lovers meeting for a secret rendezvous.

The floor is weak and won't take a lot of time to cut through, with the right equipment. With what we have, though, the going is slow and agonizing. The hardest part proves to be the end pieces, perfect circles that need to be large enough for Martha to squeeze through, and us to remove and reinsert, but small enough to make it easier to conceal. With the trash cans further concealing the outside cap, I feel sure we have enough time to execute the plan before detection.

The first week we are strong. Bob catches the flu and is out of commission for the next few. We work our tails off the following few weeks to make up time. By the eighteenth week, after so much hard work that I sometimes thought would be beyond us, and almost being caught a number of times, we have cut all the way through.

I stand and clap my hands together and watch the dust fall. Bob is on his knees rearranging the matting he had placed there to collect the debris from our efforts. Now, we both lift it up and empty its contents into the john. Bob stretches, straightens himself and flushes the toilet. He observes the tunnel. I then grab the inside cap and place it down into the hole. It looks good. We shift the bookshelf to complete the disguise. Now it looks perfect, just as I imagined it.

Bob makes his way toward his bed, where Martha rests, and sits down beside her. He moves the top of the bed but it doesn't disturb her. He rubs the back of her neck hard, which she obviously enjoys. I lean up against the opposite wall. Bob notices my self satisfaction.

"You must be pretty proud of yourself."

I fold my arms to indicate I am. He continues on.

"You made a tunnel through my cell."

"*We* made the tunnel," I say. "The only thing left is Martha."

He looks down toward her and I can see doubt creeping into his face. It's as though Bob knew, deep down, that he couldn't deliver on his promise.

No, I think. *He wouldn't have agreed to my plan, spend all that time and energy digging the tunnel, if he knew he couldn't train her.*

He kisses her head and her ears twitch. He looks up at me. "I'm going to need some time to train her. We need to go through the tunnel, identify individual scents, and learn how to dig on command. It needs to become routine for her."

I smile. "That's why you're here."

He smiles wanly. "It's going to take some time, she needs to be focused. I can't have you here distracting her. When the time comes, she will find you."

I start to leave.

"What are you going to do in the meantime?" he asks.

I turn toward him. "Find out who placed us all here. Who did this to me. When I get out, I intend paying the leader of this organization a little visit. He won't escape my wrath."

He arches an eyebrow, then points a finger at me. "Be careful. We've come too far. Don't screw things up for us."

I nod and make my way out.

• • •

Snitches, out on the streets, aren't the ones that drive around in limos and live in big mansions. Snitches aren't on the docks loading the drugs, guns, or whatever the vice of the day is. Snitches are the ones working the streets, talking to the clients, the ones caught between the big time and the bottom of the barrel. And trying their best to have it both ways, dealing with good and bad alike.

In here, it is very much the same thing. If you look hard enough, you can find them. They aren't the ones with the fancy TV's or even the ones that helped the guards with their duties. It's those in the slop, the guy's that walk the beat and know where everything is. It's the janitors.

I watch several janitors to see if any one of them stick out. I look to see if their behavior gives them away. If any one of them had been on the streets, had been dealers. Try as they might, I can still pick them out. If I can find someone like that, they might have something to gain by giving me valuable information. Then I luck out and spot just the man I want— an old snitch of mine from the outside. I have to hope he won't remember or recognize me. I have to hope.

I need to find out how I got here, in a prison located no doubt miles outside the city. A prison that holds a myriad of people I know all to well— heck, I put most of them here—and some that I don't at all. I have millions of questions and I hope that Jack MacQuinty will have the answers. After I follow him around here and there for a couple days, today I find him milling around the dining room area. His back is to me, but somehow, I think he knows I'm there.

"I'm looking for answers, Jack."

He continues to sweep nothing into his dustpan. "Breakfast was served hours ago."

I quickly become impatient. "I'm looking for the person who brought me here. Who did this to me?"

He stops sweeping, turns to face me. "Who the heck are you, anyway?"

I decide to chance it, reveal my identity to him. I use the voice. "Surely you remember me, Jacky? You were my snitch. And now you're here. With me."

His eyes bulge open in shock, but then his expression changes quickly. He smiles at me. A horrible, smarmy grin. "You really don't know do you?"

He is soaking it up. I remain silent. He continues.

"What's in it for me, huh?"

I eye him strongly. "Money. When I get out of here, a lot of money. You know me, you know I can pay you a very large sum."

His eyes glaze over at the mention of the word money. "The building in the southeast corner, behind the toolshed. You'll find some answers there."

So, my objective becomes clear—I have to break into that building. That night, when the moon is full, I make my way down the concrete path. The towers are silent and the discs are up and active. Then, I spot a guard patrolling the yard. I proceed to sneak up behind him and hit him on the head with everything I've got. I muster enough strength to pull him under the roof's protection.

Taking his keys, I quickly make my way to the relevant building. I'm glad I can reach it without having to go near those discs. I wade through the keys and finally open the door. The inside is large and open plan in design. The smell is moldy, like bad metal and old papers. There are filing cabinets, hundreds of them, and if I was a betting man I would bet that these are inmate records. Paper backups of their computer files, no doubt. The cabinets are marked and I can easily find what I'm looking for.

I open the cabinet and find my name. I stare at it for a while, touching it softly as if it is a fragile object. I blink, trying to make sense of the name there. It is at once memorable and instantly forgettable at the same time, almost like it's mine but it isn't. I shrug the bizarre feeling off. I haven't heard that name in a long time, I tell myself. The drugs they've fed me here, the deprivation. Full recognition slowly begins to kick in. I pull the records out and go through them. Whoever brought me here knew my identity, but kept it safe from my allies and enemies here.

Who is behind all this? Who put me here?

My mind races as I go through a list of suspects. I have so many enemies—the list is a long one. But who would want to play with me like this? To break me? Who would go to such elaborate lengths to keep me here, in secret? Of all my myriad enemies, this was the style of only one of them—Robert Latham. The Cobra, were he alive, would not resort to such mind tricks. There are others. Many others. But none would resort to such intricate games as this. This has Latham written all over it.

Has he indeed learned my identity then? It would seem so, and that terrifies me.

I try to push it from my mind and continue.

I look around for anything else of interest. In the back of the room, I find another door. Locked. Again going through the keys, I open it and find a small storage room. I see my name again, tagged to a moldy bag. Inside it is my costume. At least, I think it's my costume. It looks as it should except it's...cheap somehow? I take it out like I am handling a baby and I bring it to my nose. The smells bring it all back to me...

• • •

I needed to keep breathing. Criminals seemed to be getting faster as I was getting slower. The psycho-adrenaline drug that was coursing through the suspect's veins wasn't helping the situation either. Adrenaline was a fantastic tool; it seemed to make you run faster, fight stronger, and become almost impenetrable to pain.

Once in a blue moon you would get reports of a person outrunning the police in an almost inescapable situation or of a man lifting more than he could possibly ordinarily do so. From the beginning, I was taught to balance adrenaline with common sense, learn to sometimes use it to my advantage or ignore it as I saw fit. That training had served me well.

Days earlier, I had busted into one of Robert Latham's human guinea pig experiments on Metro's west side. His plan was to sell his adrenaline drugs out on the streets, like P.C.P., but this drug would give its victim an unhealthy shot of adrenaline, along with an unwieldy concoction of other chemicals. All to make it that much more potent and addictive. Try as I might, Latham was able to escape again, as did at least half the shipment. Now the filthy drug was out on the streets of my city and I've been running down criminals for the past four weeks.

I chased the perp down an alley and caught him at the dead end. I grabbed him by the back of the collar and stood him up, then whipped him around and forced him against the wall. Panicked, he threw his hands at me, spitting and scratching. He began to shake; slowly at first, they quickly became more pronounced, then violent. His body heaved, his brain began to explode in his skull. There was nothing I could do but ease his fall down into the wet snow. This was the eighth such incident this week. That fact alone sickened me to my core.

I then noticed the headlights shining on my back. From the height of them, it was a van or truck. I stood up, intending to use my grapnel and line for escape, but...they weren't in my belt. Had Max forgotten to place them back there? Then, out of nowhere, a punch was thrown and I hit the ground hard. Two men were standing next to me. I found out later their names were Chevy and Mac. A trench coat came down to their shoes. The Trenchcoat Mafia. I jumped to my feet, launched myself at Chevy, landing on top of him. Mac ran up behind me, but I managed to send him flying with a kick. I began to wail on Chevy's face—there would be time to talk later. I was too focused on Chevy, I forgot about Mac.

He jumped me from behind and picked me up. He had my arms pinned behind my back. As I tried to push him against the wall, the wounded Chevy approached me. I used Mac as leverage and I managed to connect with a kick, sending Chevy off balance. He then reached into his coat pocket as I banged Mac's body against the wall. Chevy produced a tazer. He shot it at me but I spun around in time, dodging the blast. The needles landed in Mac's back and he fell, releasing me. I ran to Chevy and landed a strong punch to his face. I grabbed him before he fell.

"Who sent you!" I growled.

A third man, I never found out who, appeared and knocked me down from behind. Before I could react, he and Chevy had produced clubs and proceeded to beat me about the head with them. My old friend adrenaline kept me from passing out as I swung my hand behind me. My blow missed and I then felt a club to my legs. I cried out in agony, my right kneecap felt like it had burst, and I fell.

They continued beating me until I couldn't possibly fight back. I should have been more careful. I was right, though. It was a van. Perfectly egg shell white in hue. They threw me into the back of it, as I clutched my right leg in pain.

$$\bullet \; \bullet \; \bullet$$

I spend most of the next morning in bed as I am feeling a little under the weather. Must have been too much excitement last night.

I hear the clank of the cell doors open; the slide is very forceful so I suppose someone is angry. I don't even roll over; it really annoys people when you don't acknowledge them. Hands grab my shoulders and yank me out of bed. I hit the ground hard.

"Careful, Charles."

The warden stands in the back and looks to see if anyone saw Chuck rough me up. Even if someone did, they wouldn't talk. I sit on the ground, a disheveled mess, and I haven't even had breakfast yet. The two men stand on opposite sides of the warden as he crouches down in front of me.

"You gonna tell me about that little incident last night?"

I decide to play dumb with him, see what kind of cards he plays. I don't say anything. He looks up at his guards and smiles in a frustrated way.

"We know it was you that broke into our records facility. We know you took your costume. I just want to know where you've stashed it."

Let's see how far I can push this.

"Have you checked up your butt?"

He nods and the other guards begin to toss the room. They won't find it here.

"I just want you to know that you are protected here," the warden said. "*We* know your secret, but I would hate for someone else here to find out. To find your costume...you know, with the variety of characters we have here."

I look at him, stare him down.

"You remember who your friends and enemies are don't you? There are enough crazies here who would want to rip you another ass." The warden grins as he says it.

He's trying to psych me out. But I won't tell him anything. He calls his sheep back.

"That's enough."

He pulls out a syringe and holds it in front of me. "You know what this is don't you?"

I knew what it was as soon as he pulled it out. Haloperidol. This was the one thing I feared. If I'm injected with it too often, I feared for my mind. I might become a dribbling idiot like so many others in this place. All my plans for escape would then be lost.

"Haloperidol," I mutter.

He pulls the syringe closer to his face, squirts a bit of the liquid out. I start to get up. The guards grab me. I struggle briefly, but after all my recent exertions, I have little strength left.

The warden smiles. "Calm down. This is meant to help you."

I fight harder but the more I fight the harder the guards hold me down. They pick me up and toss me on my bed, on my back. One of them rolls my sleeve up. I feel the sharp needle enter my arm. I continue to struggle, but everything becomes hazy, muddled.

And I am gone.

• • •

Squeaking wheels wake me in the middle of the night. I turn to see what the commotion is all about. One of the guards, Carl, enters my cell and notices that I am awake.

"Go back to sleep," he urges.

I ignore him as I continue to watch silently, not moving in my bed. The second guard wheels in my new roommate, a man on a gurney. Carl comes over and sits on my bed, crushing my legs. I stare right at him.

"Mr. Ray is going to be your new roommate."

I remain silent but continue staring.

"I want you to be nice to Mr. Ray. He had a stroke."

I don't say anything. Carl looks up at the other guard and they leave.

I avert my attention to Mr. Ray as I hear the cell door clank shut and the guards walk away. I throw the sheets off and I start to move. The floor is cold on my feet as I shuffle my way over to my new cellmate.

There are two bars on both sides of his bed, so he can't roll out. I put my hands on the bars as I peer down at him. He doesn't move, just stares up at me blinking his eyes, one side of his face drooped below the other.

"Can you speak?" I ask.

He continues blinking, faster than usual. There's an active mind in there, I feel sure, but his body has failed him. I pity him.

The next day is the same as all the others. I shuffle through it like a zombie, moving here and there within the compound. I wonder how Bob is coming along with Martha's training. Strange how I miss the old guy.

When the time comes, I decide to eat my supper out here in the open, at a table outside the cafeteria and in front of the long, covered walkway. I miss the night sky sometimes. Miss flying through it on my grapnel and line. There is a cool chill in the air and it freezes the nerves. I look over to the wall lined with the water-filled trash cans. Nothing is visible. I can't help but smile.

Martha comes up to me. She sits beside me, eyeing my vegetable lasagna. Bob approaches, too, and sits down as I feed Martha some of my dinner. It feels good to see him, but he's nervous. I don't like the look of that.

"We need a backup plan," he says.

"CALM DOWN. THIS IS MEANT TO HELP YOU."

I wipe my hands off, pick up my fork, and continue to eat. "This is our plan. No backup is needed."

He is clearly concerned. "We have to come to the possibility that this isn't going to work. What happens if it doesn't work?"

I continue to eat, not worried. "It *will* work. It has to."

"She found you now, one man among a hundred. Out there...out there it is one woman among millions. What if she gets lost? Gets scared or waylaid?"

I am bored with this. "If she gets lost or scared, then she'll come back. She will come back to you. And we'll be stuck here forever."

He wipes his mouth. "Why don't we dig the tunnel further underground, under the whole darn thing?"

I put down my fork in frustration. "You've seen the blueprints, you know there is a grid pattern of lasers underneath that soil." I point out to the dusty yard area. "You know we can't get past those, right? Not even underground. And they go right up until the fence. At bedtime, the discs pop up. If one hundred pounds or more of constant pressure is applied to one, the alarms go off. This dog weighs less than that. She can't make her way through the fence in broad daylight; the guards would see and put a stop to it. But at night, under the cover of darkness, she makes her way across, squeezes through the gap in the fence, she's out. She is our only plan."

He looks away and then looks back at me. "Why don't we make a run for it one day? We just make a run."

He's clutching at straws and not getting the point.

"They will get us, don't you understand that? This goop here they're feeding us is to make us weak. The protein blocker is everywhere, it's all designed to make us so weak that we can't make a run for it." I sigh. "My strength is waning each day."

He slams his hand down on the table. "Okay, okay. We'll do this."

I smile.

He stands up and points his finger at me. I am not threatened. "You better make damn well sure this works."

I pick up my fork and continue to eat. He begins to walk away.

Later, after dinner and some more fun at bingo, I slip out into the night, and make my way to the trash cans where the exit of our tunnel is. In one of the cans, which I'd emptied of its water earlier, I have a small box secreted. I check if there's anyone around before removing it and hurry inside. I walk toward Bob's cell as fast as I can, hoping that no one will see me. It's a risk I have to take.

"I found something."

Bob turns toward me and sees me standing in his doorway. He keeps watch as I walk into his cell holding the box before me. His cell is neater now than it was before. His bookshelf looks more organized. His tools for training Martha are here if you know where to look. Doggie treats, some of my clothes, and evidence of scratch marks cover the floor. I'm heartened by this.

"I see the training is a success."

He shakes his head. "We're not even half way there. She can find out a scent, and crawl through that tunnel but she still has to make it through that fence out there and all the way to the city and your Leena."

I put the box up on the table.

"What's that?" he asks.

I remove the lid and throw it onto the floor. Martha's ears perk up as it crashes. Bob moves over to look inside. He sees my costume and lets out a gasp.

"Holy...! You're The...The..."

Ignoring him, I then take out the scarf that I bought Leena. It is worn but I can still smell her perfume on it. She only wore it on the most special of occasions. At other times, I often kept it with me for good luck. I must have had it in my belt when the Mafia apprehended me.

"This is our ticket out of here. Leena's scarf."

My hand trembles as I hand it to him. Bob takes it and a look of incredulity overcomes him.

"How did you get this? And that suit?"

"From the building behind the toolshed. They've got files on all of us there."

He whistles in astonishment, then smiles. "I will train Martha to smell this, to ingrain the scent into her memory. She will find your Leena, I guarantee this. So long as she isn't waylaid, you will be a free man. We both will be."

He nods as he says this. I don't know if he really believes that or if it is the Parkinson's.

"Thank you, old friend."

We embrace. I pet Martha and leave.

Before bedtime, I make an effort to see Mattie. This could well be the last time I see him. I sit with him in his cell as we exchange bug bags and compliment each other on our finds. I've noticed that he's been acting strangely the last few times I saw him. His nerves appear at boiling point. I decide to ask him what the problem is. I sit on his bed as he sits at his desk and he looks through my bag.

"Now partner, what's this?" He pulls up a bug's head out of my bag.

"Praying mantis," I identify.

He looks up, shocked. "Damn son, how did you get a hold of that?"

I smile. "Rose bushes. In the garden outside. They eat aphids."

He chuckles and smacks his leg. Sadness then overwhelms him.

"What's wrong, Mattie?" I ask.

He smiles wanly. "They got me with the 'H'."

I never told him that I had recently as well. He perks up.

"Guess what I did?"

I drop the subject.

He goes over to his bookshelf and pulls out a newspaper article. "I stole a newspaper from the library. That'll teach 'em."

He throws the article on my lap. My heart skips a beat.

The Wraith.

Missing For Weeks.

Leena must have been out there looking for me all this time. Max, too. They would never think to look here, though, wherever exactly here is.

"You ain't no ordinary detective are you?"

I smile. "No, Mattie, I'm not."

I leave him and finally head to my own cell. It'll be bedtime soon, and some hours later, Bob will let Martha loose. And, before too long, I'll be home again.

My mind is in a daze. At some point, I find myself sitting on the floor. It feels as though I fell some time ago. Margaret, the woman from the dance, comes in.

"Hey, handsome, mind if I sit a while?"

I don't say anything. She sits down beside me on the floor and puts her arm around me.

"How did we get to this?"

I lower my head. I have no idea what she is talking about, but for the first time since I've been here, she begins to look somewhat familiar to me.

"I know it's been hard since they found out about you. I couldn't believe it myself, to tell the truth. I thought I truly knew you."

She squeezes my shoulder. It feels good, but her words leave me completely confused.

"Everything we did. It was just a job, a job we did to the best of our ability. Now our job is to survive, any way we can. You hear me?"

She squeezes my shoulder again.

"You think about that," she says.

She gets up and makes her way out of the room.

"I am striving for life. You need to as well."

She turns to me and blows me a kiss.

• • •

Bob sits on his bed, hands on his lap, looking down at the ground. Martha is lying beside him. She is sleeping.

"It's time," he says softly to himself.

Bob looks over to his beloved Martha. She still sleeps. He gazes lovingly at her, his angel. He softly calls her name; she wakes up and goes over to him like she hasn't seen him in years. He pets her and kneels down in front of her, taking her in his arms.

After a few moments, he slides his bookshelf aside and removes the cap. He lights a candle he had earlier procured from the tool shed. He crawls through the narrow, dingy tunnel and slowly makes his way to the end of it, deftly pushing out the cap there and moving the empty trash can to one side ever so slightly. Back he goes, and soon comes out in his cell once again, where Martha sits resolutely waiting for him. They are together, potentially, for the last time. Even in his most confident of moments, he knows the chances of Martha reaching her destination are slim. But, he also knows there is no turning back now.

He reaches into his pocket, pulls out the note he had been given and Leena's scarf. He attaches the note to her collar and puts the scarf to her nose, allowing her to get a good, long whiff of it. He throws the scarf on the ground and gently grabs her face, makes her look him in the eyes.

"You find Leena, you hear me? You find her."

The dog tries to lick his face. He begins to tear up.

"You get lost, you get scared, you come back to me." He tightens his grip. "You come back to me." He shakes her head. "You hear me?"

He hugs her. He lets her go and she starts off into the tunnel. He sticks the scarf behind some books in his shelf, replaces the cap at both ends and then moves the bookshelf back into position.

He flops down on his bed and weeps.

This is it. No turning back.

• • •

I glanced at her from time to time as I tried to focus on the job at hand. I was seated at the communications terminal in the Lair as she approached me. The white bathrobe flowed open as the belt around Leena's waist loosely tied it to her. Her black panties and bra with white outer lacing peeked out from time to time as she slowly made her way toward me.

As she neared, for a moment I wasn't in the Lair anymore, and the gorgeous creature approaching me wasn't Leena. But who was she? Who?

She bent down and kissed me on the forehead, then the lips. Her luscious, full lips felt heavenly on mine. She handed me a cup of coffee. I handed her a small package, a white box tied with a ruby red lace ribbon and bow.

"For me?" she asked teasingly.

She shook as she opened the box and lifted from it its contents. It was a scarf. A lovely, blue silk scarf.

But that wasn't Leena, and we weren't in the Lair. For a brief moment, clarity of thought was achieved. That wasn't Leena.

It was Margaret.

• • •

The plan fails. As Margaret and I are having breakfast together in the cafeteria the next morning, Martha comes bounding up to her and points her right leg at her. The faithful dog has found her quarry. The scarf had been Margaret's all the time.

The sirens are blaring as I run down the hall. Nothing makes any sense to me now. Who is Leena? Who is Margaret? Who am I? I don't know anymore. Lights are flashing, almost blinding me. There was no plan B. There was no fallback option. I put everything into this. This one plan. It was going to be our ticket out of here. All I can do now is run as fast as I can for the front entrance. I can still make this escape. I have to.

The warden and several guards follow behind me, screaming at me to stop. I barge past those officials in front of me. Nothing is going to stop me now. However, they slowed me down enough for the warden and the others to catch up to me. I am at the entrance, so close to freedom, just a few more steps. One of my pursuers jumps me and falls on top of me. I am now on the ground, with the man and the others now barreling on top. I try to struggle but my strength is gone. What little I had left was spent in my flight. All hope is lost. It's over.

The front door opens and, by some miracle, Leena is there, standing in the doorway. She looks on in shock as the guards attempt to restrain me.

"Leena. Help me, please. Leena!"

The guards slip a straitjacket on me and drag me away from the love of my life. She stands there, motionless, watching me, but she does nothing. I could swear I see a tear roll down her cheek as I disappear around the corner and away from her forever.

• • •

"He's suffering from pugilist dementia, Miss Patterson."

Leena Patterson was ensconced within Dr. Burton's office. Dr. Jack Burton, a middle-aged man with bushy brown hair, greying at the temples, and striking hazel eyes, was the Metro City Mental Care Unit's Chief Medical Officer. It was at this facility that Paul Sanderson and Leena had committed the hapless Brendan Jones a few years prior.

"As you know, he was committed here suffering intense delusions that he was some sort of 'superhero.' But, with the aid of medication, he was controllable most of the time, and often quite calm. In recent times, however, he has worsened appreciably. He now thinks he is in a prison and has tried to escape on numerous occasions."

She looked at him with some sadness.

"Why is it that you decided to check up on him today, Miss Patterson? You're not a relative are you?" Dr. Burton enquired.

"My fiancé and I actually admitted him to your fine facility, before you transferred here," Leena explained. "We found him on the streets, dressed in a homemade Wraith costume, trying to beat up some poor homeless people. As you know, my fiancé Paul Sanderson takes a great interest in charity work and helping those less fortunate than ourselves. I wanted to see how Mr. Jones was coming along. I'm sad to see not well."

"Well," Dr. Burton said with a sigh, "we've tried to facilitate his treatment as best we can, but he's become a complete nightmare. He's recently broken into our backup records facility, which we then secured. Nevertheless, he assaulted an orderly and broke in, stealing some personal effects. He constantly smashes up his room. He now has violent mood swings, rages, attacking several of my orderlies, some brutally. Just a couple of months ago, he sent one of them to the hospital, requiring intensive plastic reconstructive surgery. He perpetually influences Mr. Bob, another of our patients, and induces his assistance in his escape efforts. What you just witnessed was his latest attempt."

"I see."

Dr. Burton looked at her carefully. "As I said, his condition has worsened appreciably. He's clumsy, often falls down. He has mood swings and now tremors. Some on the board have argued for padded cell enclosure, but I've always thought if we were able to nail down the right medication, we could control him and still allow him some measure of contact with the rest of the patient population. I've always considered that an important aspect of care and treatment, hence most of the patients here are allowed to roam the compound at will; within reason, of course. I am loathe to give up on that approach. I've recently tried to help ease his symptoms with Haloperidol, a specialist medication for dementia, but it looks as though this has only made things worse. I'm afraid I now have to concur with my colleagues. A padded cell is the best place for him and for those around him. We'll continue with a regular regimen of medication and hope we can at least make him more comfortable."

She smiled weakly. There wasn't much more she could say. "So, there's no hope?"

"I'm afraid not. He's nearing the end stretch, though there's no way of telling how long it will take. Weeks, months perhaps. There's only so much the mind and body can take. All we can do now is try to make him as comfortable as possible."

He tried to smile, but Leena could tell this was tough going for him, too. He obviously cared, about Jones and everyone else within his facility.

"Thank you very much for this opportunity, Dr. Burton. I'm just sorry the news is so sad," Leena said, standing.

"It's never easy, this sort of situation. Not for anyone involved. We'll take good care of him, Miss Patterson. He won't be hurting anyone else, nor himself, from now on, I assure you. I'll let you know if there's any change in his condition."

Leena smiled and bade him farewell. She walked slowly through the facilities corridors and out into the parking lot. There stood Paul Sanderson, leaning up against their damaged Bentley Continental GT.

"How is he?" he asked.

"Not good. He still thinks he's you, but now he's gotten violent, and continually tries to escape. He was attempting just such an escape when I entered the building. He recognized me, begged me for help."

"I'm sorry, Leena," Paul said, placing an arm around her. "I didn't know he was in such bad shape."

"I still don't understand how he came to think he's you."

"To be honest, I don't really know myself," Paul said, squinting as he tried to remember. "When I came across him and his partner Hatchet Margaret making a hit in that TV store drug front, I was in the process of enveloping him with my Judgment Stare when Margaret threw a hatchet at me. I evaded it, but it flew through the energies of the Eyes of Judgment. There was something of a reaction at the time, but I thought nothing more of it as I tried to chase her down. He managed to get away, and we caught up with him later in his own version of my uniform." He rubbed his chin in thought. "I can only guess that the hatchet somehow caused some sort of a short circuit with my Judgment Stare and in some manner he acquired a fraction of my memories."

"Amazing," she said under her breath. She looked at him closely. "I know he was evil, that he committed such acts of attrocity over the years as an assassin, but...I can't help but feel sorry for him. In a way, he's now you. It was as though I could see a portion of you in him. His desperation in there just...broke my heart."

"We'll make sure he continues to get the very best of care. Come on. After what we've been through in Little England these past few weeks, I want to go home. There's nothing more we can do here."

He escorted Leena to her side of the car and helped her inside. She watched as he took one last look at the looming building, its graying white-washed walls dominating all around them, then entered the car himself.

And they were off. Home.

The End

Sundown...a new sort of Wraith story

$\mathcal{S}$*undown* has an interesting tale behind it. Originally, it was a story which I was going to publish myself in a future edition of *The Wraith Adventures* series of books. A longtime friend and member of my online forum, Adam Oravec, has long wanted to be a writer, and I thought a short Wraith story would be ideal practice for him. When he submitted his completed story to me, I was at once intrigued and taken aback at the same time. In its original form, it was a very violent, often crude story with an ending that made little sense and was depressing in the extreme. Even if viewed as a sort of 'Elseworlds' story, it couldn't be printed as it was. And yet, the idea behind the story, the overriding plot, was an excellent one, and one which I praised Adam highly for. After reading through it, I suggested several ideas which would solve the inherent problems within the story, but Adam felt incapable of applying those ideas to his story. Not wanting to abandon the story entirely, I decided to step in.

The idea behind *Sundown*, that of The Wraith being down and out, incarcerated in an insane asylum and desperately planning his escape, really fired my imagination. I've never attempted such a story myself, especially not in the first person format. But there had to be a payoff at the end. There had to be a light at the end of the tunnel, some sense of hope. There must always be hope in such stories. So, I set myself the task of making the story tighter, less crude and violent and, above all, to bring it all together at the end to not only make sense, but to bring that feeling of hope to the proceedings, while still maintaining the original story's sense of loss and sadness. I think I achieved all that, but the ultimate proof of that will come from you, the reader. *You* have the final say.

I must say, I found it difficult writing in the first person. It's not a style I prefer. However, in my full rewrite, I decided to stick with it to differentiate the meat of the story with the ending. All will make sense in that regard at the end. In that context, I think the differing styles work extremely well together and help explain just what is happening. There is action aplenty, flashbacks and emotion to spare—as every good pulp story should. As a note to regular Wraith readers, this story takes place immediately after the events of the novels *Cry of the Werewolf* and *Swamp Witch of Satan's Forest*. You don't need to read those stories to be able to understand *Sundown*, but the events of the former two are mentioned at the end of the latter.

To finish, I'd just like to thank a few people. Firstly, to Ron Fortier, for agreeing to run with my idea of an anthology of Wraith short stories. Thank you, Ron, you're the best. To Adam Oravec, for coming up with the idea for *Sundown* and inspiring me to complete it. To my fellow writers in this anthology, Bobby, Greg and Sean. Thanks for agreeing to come on this ride with me. I hope you enjoyed it and had fun in the murky world of the Dread Avenger of the Underworld. To my wife, Jennifer and my family. Thanks for always being there. And thank you, my dear readers, for staying with me over the years and enjoying my little adventure stories. It is for you, after all, that I do what I do. Thanks one and all.

FRANK DIRSCHERL (b. 1973) is a professionally certified library technician and has been working in libraries since 1992. Over the years he has also covered and packed books and other material for a book wholesale company, been an online journalist, worked as a data assistant at an E.N.T. surgery and as a lecturer to children on the merits of the comic book. His written work includes *The Wraith* (filmed in 2005), *Valley of Evil, Cult of the Damned, Cry of the Werewolf,* the non-fiction *The Wraith: Eyes of Judgment - The Official Script Book & Movie Guide* (with Stephen Semones) and more. He lives on the south coast of NSW, Australia with his wife Jennifer, where he's currently working on his next Wraith novel amongst other works of fiction.

For more information on Frank and The Wraith, please visit **www. frankdirscherl.com** and **www.trinitycomics.com**

ADAM ORAVEC (b. 1980) is a computer programmer and has been working in this field since 2005. Prior to this, he worked in the retail industry. His hobbies include film, theatre, writing and reading. He has written one spec script, *The Days of Christopher Robin. Sundown* is his first published work. He lives in Charlotte, NC.

TALES OF THE SHADOW LEGION

The superheroes of Nocturne, Florida, known as the Shadow Legion, are back but this time each is going solo. In a quartet of new adventures, each must confront weird and bizarre threats to their city and its people.

The blind Ferryman, who communes with ghosts, must save an innocent child from an eternal nightmare while the battling Nightbreaker confronts an old foe from his past with the ability to rain down death and destruction on the city. Meanwhile the Black Talon is kidnapped by a powerful necromancer whose obsession is to destroy all superheroes. And finally the beautiful Dreamcatcher must ally herself with a bizarre living rag-doll in her search for a maniacal fiend.

Here are four fast paced adventures chronicling the exploits of amazing heroes in their eternal battle with the forces of darkness. The Shadow Legion fights on.

VOLUME 2

SHADOW LEGION
NIGHTMARE CITY

THOMAS DEJA

AN AIRSHIP 27 PRODUCTION
AIRSHIP27HANGAR.COM
New PULP

www.ingramcontent.com/pod-product-compliance
Lightning Source LLC
Chambersburg PA
CBHW031201260626
47169CB00004B/1200